COMING HOME TO FEATHERWOOD FALLS

FEATHERWOOD FALLS SERIES
BOOK 5

HEATHER REYBURN

For my Family
Thank you for your unwavering support and
encouragement.
I love and value you all.

1

***

As a golden glimmer of autumn daylight filtered through a gap in the curtains, the deafening notes of The Proclaimers' "I'm Gonna Be (500 Miles)" blasted from the phone, causing it to dance around the bedside table and shocking Briony Shepherd into an upright position. After snatching up her fiancé's device, she shook Alex awake, tapped the green icon, and pressed it against his sleep-crumpled ear, mouthing, 'It's your mum.'

Alex rose on one elbow, meeting Briony's worried frown as he mumbled a "hello".

With the time difference between Scotland and Australia foremost in her mind, a call at this hour could only spell bad news.

Alex touched the speaker icon and his mother's broad Scottish accent filled the room.

'So ... if you want to see him before he passes, you'd better get on a plane now.'

Briony tilted her head in question as Alex murmured, 'Grandpa.'

She nodded understandingly in the quiet; voices blurring as unease lodged in her throat.

It had been one of the worst months she could remember. On one of the rare nights she finished at the hotel early, Alex had organised a lift home with another staff member, and she had gone shopping. Minutes from home, while she sat waiting for the lights to change, two thugs had attempted to carjack her, smashing the driver's side mirror when they couldn't open the locked door. She had accelerated forward with a lurch as the green light appeared and sped to the relative safety of their rented home, shaking with terror and with barely a glance behind her to check if the youths had run off or fallen under a following vehicle. Still not over her shock, days later an unexpected storm had blown in from the sea while no one was in the house—drenching her brand-new laptop while it sat on the table beside an open window. The burglar-proof mesh had offered no protection from the deluge, and it had cost her a fortune to have it dried and restored.

Briony's concentration fixed on Alex as his mother said, 'He's still talking a wee bit. But he's gone down quickly. The doctor says he might have a few days if we're lucky.'

Alex groaned and Briony stroked his upper arm and mouthed, 'You have to go.'

'I'm on my way.' He rubbed a hand over his golden stubble-coated jaw, said goodbye to his mother, and ended the call. 'My strong, stoic grandfather. It's hard to comprehend, but what else should I do? I want to see him again.'

'I know,' Briony said. They gazed at each other for a quiet moment before she spoke. 'You're thinking about last night, aren't you?'

He nodded as the previous evening's drama in the hotel kitchen flashed through Briony's mind.

The tirade had been between Silvio, the new senior manager, and one of the chefs. The cause trivial—a plate returned from a customer following a mix-up of the order. The issue had been easily remedied, and the customer had been kind and understanding. Silvio had not. Upsetting the rest of the team clearly wasn't something he considered, but for Alex and the three other kitchen staff, the unwarranted and over-reactive explosion had come as a shock in their previously well-oiled and friendly squad.

'I don't want to leave you, especially with that sodding boss.' Concern wrinkled Alex's freckled face.

'I'll be fine.' Briony hugged him, determined to hide her own fear. 'Once you're on the way to Scotland,

I'll talk to him. We're due for holidays, so I'm sure your absence for a few days will be fine,' Briony said, crossing her fingers behind her back as she spoke.

Wide awake now, she grasped the laptop off the table, and hopped back into bed.

Within minutes, with the flight booked, they began throwing clothes into a bag.

'Six hours before departure sounded like heaps of time, but it's not, is it?' Alex said, his blue eyes dark with anxiety.

Briony shook her head. 'No. Let's eat and then get on the road. Hopefully the peak-hour gridlock will have cleared by then.'

Alex grimaced. The highway between the Gold Coast and Brisbane airport was notoriously frantic and, despite the multiple lanes, the traffic crawled to a standstill no matter the time or weather.

As they gathered the essential passport and coat from the cupboard, silent fear engulfed Briony. She breathed slowly, certain Alex would hear her pounding heart as dread roiled inside her.

Coping with his grandfather's passing would be a struggle for Alex, but explaining his absence to the new manager filled Briony with terror.

∽

With two hours to spare, Briony drove into the airport car park. Adrenaline had fuelled their mad scatter, but now the panic faded and reality set in. Her relationship with Alex had been tested for three years, starting with pandemic restrictions and then their separation when Briony returned to Australia without Alex. When he could finally travel without having to spend their life savings, he'd arrived in Sydney where Briony had been waiting, believing their worries were over.

Several short-lived hospitality jobs had followed, and their love deepened before they found employment in the high-end Surfers Paradise hotel—their perfect combination of Alex's chef skills and Briony's marketing expertise ensuring a warm welcome and good wages. The hours were long and demanding, but they had become used to the challenges and enjoyed the friendly team at the hotel—until Silvio arrived and rapidly took the shine off the entire situation.

Alex dropped his bag on the ground and reached for Briony. As his arms wrapped around her, she pressed her face against the hollow between his collarbone and neck, fighting back tears. Her reliance on the big, strong Scotsman who had stolen her heart surprised her. She found reassurance in his loyalty and positive outlook on all that was thrown their way—and now, when her vulnerability was higher than ever, he was leaving again.

It's just a minor hitch, she told herself. A bump in the road. But one as important to Alex as it would be for Briony if it were her in his place.

As though reading her unspoken thoughts, Alex slid his hands up to her cheeks and held her gently as they kissed. 'I'll do whatever I have to for Mum and Dad and be back as soon as I can. Okay?'

'Okay.' She gave him a watery smile, meeting his kind eyes and reassuring grin as he rubbed a hand through his straw-coloured hair.

They walked toward the terminal, pausing at the overhead sign to confirm the flight details, and in less than half an hour they hovered beside the "Passengers only" sign.

'See you soon,' he said, then planted a last kiss on her lips and stepped onto the escalator.

Her gaze never shifted as he disappeared out of sight. With sagging shoulders, she trailed back to the car.

The return trip to the Gold Coast was uneventful, the peak hour traffic cleared and the autumn sun shining. But Briony felt conflicted.

The beach was lovely, their comfortable shared house convenient and inexpensive by Gold Coast standards, despite the too-loud music played by their housemates when they were trying to sleep after a late shift. Balancing the current toxic undercurrent floating through the hotel staff with the positives of living on the coast had become hard enough, particularly as she reminisced about her days living on the Isle of Skye. She would be thirty soon and desperately missed country life. Since returning to Australia, they had both loved being able to dress in light clothing, soak up the sun almost every day of the year, and enjoy the casual, beachy lifestyle. But now, did the call for Alex to return to Scotland signal the end of the life they thought they wanted? She wasn't sure.

PREPARED FOR SILVIO'S OUTBURST, Briony stared, mesmerized by the fury oozing from his every pore. She'd read about people frothing at the mouth, spittle forming around their lips, but had never actually witnessed it. Now she bit back a hysterical giggle as his face deepened to a shade of puce while he ranted.

Thumping a fist on the counter, he shouted, 'How dare he go without discussing the issue with me first.'

It was on the tip of her tongue to say they would have if urgency hadn't prevailed, but she decided against it, fearing it would make matters worse. Instead, she clamped her teeth together and remained mute.

'I will have his wages completed today and he will not be welcome here again.'

Briony's mind raced. While they were "casual

employees" and therefore subject to immediate dismissal, both had dedicated six months of long, hard hours to ensuring the smooth running of the business. They'd believed their efforts were valued and appreciated until the supposedly vibrant and experienced Silvio joined the staff. Even if they had been before, now they were not.

Her shock and fascination at Silvio's reaction rapidly turned to disappointment and then anger as her thoughts spun. Her instincts had been right. She and Alex had both given their all—and this was their thanks.

She nodded, her voice firm but quiet as she fought to control her rage. 'Fine. While you're arranging for Alex's termination, you can do mine too. I am giving my notice from this moment—and will put it in writing if you require it.'

Shooting him a challenging stare, she lifted her chin, spun around, and strode out of the room.

BRIONY CHECKED HER WATCH. Alex would be in the air by now. Should she send him a message? They had wi-fi on the plane. She chewed her lip as the urge faded. The last thing he needed was more stress. She would wait until he reached Scotland. With the anger now abating, leaving her determined but resigned to her decision, she picked up her phone and dialled her mother.

'Hello?'

Briony let her shoulders slump at the sound of her mother's cheery tone. 'Hi, Mum. How are you?'

'I'm fine. We're all fine.' Ginny paused. 'But I can tell from your voice that you are not.'

Briony took a deep breath and relayed the day's events, beginning with the phone call from Scotland and ending with the diatribe from the manager. 'So ... we're now officially unemployed and I'm not sure what to do?' she ended with an unsuccessful attempt to quell her quavering voice.

'Don't worry, love. Everything will work out for the best. What's the situation with your house? Are you tied to the lease, or can you leave?'

Ginny Shepherd was a strong, caring woman—and an insightful mother.

Briony cleared her throat, her mother's practical tones easing her anxiety. 'No. It's Angela and Mark's home. We pay them room rent, so I guess we could leave at any time—even if I have to give them extra while they find another tenant.'

'Right then. The answer is simple. Check with the payroll people at your workplace and ensure you've followed procedure. Talk to Angela and Mark and sort out what their needs are—and then come home to the farm.'

Briony straightened as the weight lifted. Of course, she always had an option—she'd just temporarily forgotten it in her quest for independence. Featherwood Station was her childhood home and would always be there for her, no matter what life threw her way.

'Thanks, Mum.' Her mouth lifted in a faint smile. 'I'll nip back to the hotel with my written resignation and talk to the others when they get home from work. Then I'll let you know.'

'Perfect. We'll see you soon,' Ginny finished.

Briony faced the window, blinking as an enormous dog dragged its screaming owner past the front fence at a gallop. Suddenly, the familiar peace of the Featherwood Falls homestead and all it contained became her goal. Beyond that, Briony couldn't think and didn't care. She was tired. Her brain was weary, and she craved the peaceful company of her mother.

'Yes. If all goes well, I'll be home at the end of the week.'

2

—————

Sophie Cunningham settled the anaesthetised dog into its crate and retreated to the operating theatre to clean up. The knot in her stomach had tightened as the day passed—not only from her mother's frantic, early-morning call, but due to the one she would make before the day was out.

Rain drummed against the animal hospital windows, falling in heavy sheets across the car park. The deluge made it impossible to see how many vehicles were left, and with only a few minutes before her lunchbreak, she decided not to go for her routine walk in this weather. Much better to sit out the back with a book and her sandwich where it was warm and filled with the familiar scents of animals, disinfectant, and freshly washed towels.

Having spent four years at the busy Inverness practice, Sophie was unfazed by almost everything that came through the clinic doors—from seriously injured animals of all breeds, shapes, and sizes, to simple health checks and vaccinations. Her work filled her heart, her senses, and her soul, and she spent long hours doing what she loved, even if it had rankled her latest boyfriend.

'Just popping into the recovery room to eat my sandwich.'

Olivia, the junior vet nurse, looked up from where she was scrubbing the instruments and reassembling them in the sterilizer. 'Okay. All good. Paul won't be back from the foaling for a couple of hours, and we've only got one cat spay left. Julia and I can manage.'

Squatting next to the sleeping labrador, Sophie pulled out her phone and cast her eye down the list of messages. Fourteen texts—all from Peter. He was hard-going. Needy. She was tired of the messages, which she mostly ignored. But it seemed to encourage him to send more, despite her repeated explanations that unless it was something urgent, her work came first. She sighed. *I might as well talk to a brick wall.* At first his desire to communicate or be with her had touched her, especially as his texts were loving and filled with ideas for their next outing or dinner together. But six months had passed, and she'd had enough of the interruptions, the demand for control over her every movement—and him.

Jumping to her feet again, she picked up her sandwich, swung a coat over her shoulders, and ran to her car in the sluicing rain.

She snatched a towel from the back seat and dried her face. Then, steeling herself, she pulled up Peter's number and hit the green icon.

'Hi, sweetie. I knew you'd ring me as soon as you could.' Peter's voice was sugary with expectation.

'I'm not ringing for the reason you think I am.' In the moment of silence, she continued, 'Our relationship is over, and I will not be seeing you again.'

As expected, and before she ended the call, Peter's manipulating and pleading began, just as he'd done on every previous occasion when she had attempted to finish their relationship. When the abusive language began, she prodded the red icon, blocked the number, and dropped the phone in her lap, her whole body shaking.

For ten minutes, she reflected on the previous few months as she struggled to ease the fear that had paralysed her. She had made excuses for not being able to meet him—work, headaches, the need to visit her parents. They hadn't worked and now, with her grandpa seriously ill, she had hoped he would understand and she could make a clean break. She was wrong.

Conflict wasn't her thing, hating letting anyone down and, even more, avoiding arguments of any sort.

Her eldest brother, Alex, had affectionately ruffled her hair and called her a softy throughout their childhood, but she didn't care. She had found her calling— helping to save lives, particularly those of animals. And that was enough for her. The last thing she needed was a man wrecking her life.

IT WAS ALMOST CLOSING time before the senior vet returned and she could corner him in the kitchen as he washed his hands. Paul was a family man, the kind who'd never failed to ask after her parents and grand-father after meeting them at her graduation the year before.

'Hi.'

Paul grabbed the towel from the railing before facing Sophie's pale face. Winter had been long and cold, and any colour in her fair, Scottish complexion was purely from embarrassment at having to ask for time off, even if it was long overdue.

'Hi. Is everything alright?'

She shook her head. 'I'm sorry to dump this on you at short notice, but my grandpa is poorly and my brother is arriving from Australia tonight. Would it be alright if I had a few days off to go home?'

'Of course, Sophie.' His voice softened. 'We're well

staffed now, and family comes first. Take all the time you need.'

Gratitude flooded her, her spirits lifting at his kind gesture.

'Thanks. I'll let the others know—and ring you from Skye once I know how things are?'

The middle-aged face creased in an understanding smile. 'Sure. But don't worry. We've more here on the payroll than we've had for years, so you do what you need to do.'

Relief rose inside her as she raced around the clinic, shared the information with those who needed to know, gathered her coat and bag, and sprinted through the rain to her car.

ACCOMPANIED by the rhythm of windscreen wipers, two hours later, Sophie drove into Inverness Airport and parked as close as she could to the terminal. She switched off the engine and slumped against the steering wheel, her mind reeling from her conversation with Peter.

Sunshine peeped through the leaden sky as the rain cleared and she stepped out of the car. A glance toward the terminal was all she needed to wipe away any regrets as the familiar figure of her beloved brother ambled through the sliding doors, a coat slung over one shoulder and a large bag in his hand.

She waved, and seconds later was enveloped in his warm embrace. Her heart lifted and she clung to him, soaking in his familiar scent.

'Good flight?' she asked.

Alex shrugged, a rueful grin twisting his usually cheerful face. 'As good as expected.'

They rearranged Sophie's gear to find a space for his bag in the car and slid into the front seat.

Neither of them spoke as Sophie negotiated the exit and they headed west on the highway toward Dingwall. Then, as the fields and craggy hills rushed past, they settled into the easy banter born of a close sibling relationship and exchanged the events each had experienced in the previous twenty-four hours.

Alex's phone pinged. 'It's Briony.'

He pressed the phone to his ear, his smile quickly fading to a frown as he listened. Nodding, he gave Sophie a resigned grimace as he responded to Briony.

'Don't worry, love. We'll find something else. Maybe the time has come for us to look at buying that café we've talked about.'

They spoke for a brief minute before he held the phone out and stared at the screen.

'Dropped out. I'll ring her from Skye.'

'Is everything okay?'

'It looks like Briony and I are unemployed and you, my sweet sister, are footloose and fancy free.'

Sophie gasped and shot him a questioning gaze. 'Will you be home for long then, or will you be flying back to Queensland as soon as Grandpa's buried?'

'I'll stay until I feel Mum and Dad are through the worst of it ... then I'll be off. Briony's returning to Featherwood Station. Not sure what either of us will find to do there, but I love her and I love Australia, so something will work out,' Alex finished. 'What about you?'

'I suppose I'll do the same—only I'll be returning to Inverness.' Sophie paused for a moment before whispering, 'I think.'

Alex sat up straighter in the passenger seat. 'You think? What does that mean?'

'Oh, I don't know. I love my job, but this business with Peter has made me reconsider my priorities. I'm twenty-four and want to see more of the world before I settle down. Like you, I suppose.'

Alex studied her in silence before answering. 'Perhaps you should see if Paul will give you extended leave without pay and you could come back to Queensland with me?'

Sophie turned so suddenly, the little car lurched onto the rough edge of the road.

'Look out!' Alex yelled, snatching the steering

wheel as Sophie guided the vehicle back to the middle of her lane.

'Sorry,' she said, reluctant to admit she could have killed them both. 'Do you mean that?'

'What—come to Australia with me?'

'Yes.'

'Of course I do. Briony's family would welcome you, and I'm sure we'll all find work somewhere. I've been granted permanent residency, but you could get a visa to work for a while as well as having a look around the country. Now, seeing as you're keen to end our dreams and I've had a good sleep on the plane, how about we swap places and I drive from here?'

She heaved a resigned breath and eased the car to the side of the road, pulled the handbrake on, and stepped out into the cool, damp air.

HOPE GATHERED DEEP INSIDE her as Alex guided the car through Kyle of Lochalsh and onto the Skye bridge. Sophie envied her brother's courage and ability to fit in wherever he went. While she didn't have his confidence, she and Briony had formed a strong friendship before Briony had returned to Australia after the pandemic lockdowns. The more Sophie thought about it, the more Alex's suggestion appealed. Their parents had encouraged their three children to live their own lives—to work hard and follow their dreams. And they had. Alex had trained alongside the best chefs in Edinburgh before returning to Skye with Briony to manage one of the island's biggest and most popular restaurants. Hamish, the brother between Alex and Sophie, was happily married with a baby and a partnership with their father in his fishing business. And Sophie had followed her dream of working with animals. Only now, something deep inside her niggled. A need for change. Excitement. Adventure.

By the time they reached the family home on the outskirts of Broadford, she had already made her decision.

3

———

$\mathcal{B}$riony couldn't wait to talk to Alex again. Tapping impatient fingers on the steering wheel, she sighed with exasperation. She would have to be patient unless she wanted to wake the entire family. The promised daily calls had been sporadic and shorter than she wanted due to time differences and not wanting to drag him away from his family. But at least Briony knew Alex and Sophie were safely ensconced in the family's Broadford home with the bonus that both had spoken to their grandfather before he took his last breath.

She turned into the driveway leading to Featherwood Station and the solid, half-stone half-timber home she had grown up in. Slowing to a crawl, she drank in the glorious pallet of colour. An avenue of poplars lined either side of the gravelled road while the vibrant green of freshly mowed grass edged the track. Beyond the tall, graceful trees, crepe myrtles flanked the car park and entrance to the homestead, the last of their flowers forming a blanket of colour amongst the autumn leaves cascading onto the ground.

A smile spread across her face as she halted in the vehicle shed beside the house, her car dwarfed by a truck, tractor, and her mother's new four-wheel-drive. Greeted by the noise of barking dogs from kennels thirty metres away, she eased herself out of the car and retrieved a suitcase. Bags and boxes were piled high in the little Subaru—the joint accumulation of both her and Alex's belongings.

Before she reached the garden gate, Ginny was there, reaching for the suitcase while hugging her daughter one-handed.

'It's wonderful to have you home again,' Ginny breathed.

Briony's shoulders sagged, relief and exhaustion flooding through her, unable to speak for fear of allowing the welling tears to spill.

The gate squeaked and Claire, Briony's younger sister—who was half a head taller than her—bounced toward them and enveloped her in a tight squeeze, while her blonde hair, swept up in a ponytail, flicked across her sister's face and tickled her nose.

Briony blinked away the tears as she returned the

hug then stepped back and studied her sister. 'Marriage suits you. I've never seen you look so happy.'

'I admit, it's pretty good. When's the big day going to be for you and Alex?' Claire nudged Briony with an elbow as they tramped up the steps and onto the veranda.

'Give her a chance, Claire,' Ginny said. 'She hasn't got through the door yet.'

The sisters laughed. 'It's okay, Mum. I know she's joking,' Briony reassured her.

Although different in appearance, Briony and Claire were as close as sisters could be, calling each other or FaceTiming at least once a week when not living under the same roof. With the previous few years fraught with unbelievable traumas as the pandemic raged, Briony had missed the close physical contact she needed with her family. The district had encountered bushfires, wildlife theft, and the discovery of a skeleton in an old mine shaft on Featherwood Station—and with the combination of events occurring while their mother ran their large and busy sheep and cattle farm, the tight-knit family had struggled.

The accidental death of their father, Lyndon Shepherd—ruled as manslaughter—then the discovery of the property next door harbouring a drug cartel and a huge haul of methamphetamine and marijuana had topped off what Ginny, imitating Queen Elizabeth II, had called their multiple "annus horribilis". All three women had given thanks they each had a loving partner to help them through.

'Coffee, darling?' Ginny asked as she dropped Briony's bag on the polished timber floor and walked into the kitchen.

'Lovely. Thanks, Mum.'

'Me too,' Claire added. 'Hey, Bri, let's bring your gear in while Mum makes the coffee.'

Briony nodded and followed her sister onto the veranda. Something in Claire's tone suggested there was more to this than simply carting bags and boxes inside.

'I've changed my sitting room around because I hardly ever use it now,' Claire said. 'Thought you could stack anything you don't need there for the moment.'

'Okay. That'll be great.' Briony eyed her sister carefully. 'Is there something you haven't told me?'

'We-ll. Sort of. Kirk and Mum have got something they want to discuss with us.'

Briony raised an eyebrow. 'So, you're not pregnant?'

'No,' Claire spluttered. 'Nothing like that ... but a change might be in the air.'

An icy grip took hold in Briony's stomach. 'You're not moving away—just as I get here?'

'Of course not. I reckon if the police force tries to move Rhys out of Featherwood Falls, he'll mutiny—or resign.'

'So—a new house then?'

'Hmm. Maybe. Tell you later.' Claire snatched up a box from the back seat and was gone before Briony could respond.

They were on their last load before their conversation returned to Briony's stay.

'Are you home for good now?' Claire asked.

'I have no idea. Don't know what we'll do next.' Briony blew out a heavy breath. 'It'll be good to have time to think things through for a while.'

'What's happening in Scotland?'

'The funeral's tomorrow, but with the time difference, I haven't called Alex today. They'll have so much to think about, and we know what it's like when a loved member of our family passes. It's hard to talk.'

Claire shot her an empathetic smile. 'Sure is. Why don't we go for a ride? Blow some of those cobwebs away. Maybe you could ring tonight, our time?'

Briony brightened, considered Claire's suggestion for a moment, and gave her a thumbs up. 'Sounds good. They're nine hours behind us, but I'm sure I'll still be awake.' She passed the last box of crockery to Claire. 'You alright with this?'

Claire rolled her eyes. 'I reckon I'll manage to stagger up the stairs.'

They quickly stowed Alex and Briony's possessions in Briony's childhood bedroom cupboards and stacked the excess behind Claire's cane sofa.

Briony glanced around. The south-facing veranda had been enclosed decades earlier, then tidied up and refurnished to form an office-come-sitting room two years earlier for Claire to operate her graphic design business from. Prettily furnished with a large desk, small cane lounge suite, and colourful cushions and curtains, Briony could see why Claire found her creativity while working there.

Briony's stomach rumbled as the smell of melting cheese wafted down the hallway. They returned to the living room, where she gave her mother a peck on the cheek and sat down in front of steaming mugs of coffee and a plate of toasted sandwiches.

'You're a gem, mother dear.'

Ginny's brow furrowed. 'By the look of you, food hasn't been a priority for a while now.'

'Yeah, well ... it's been a busy few days—actually, make that a busy few months. It's ridiculous. We've been working in hotels for a long time, where food is constantly available, but actually finding the time and money to sit down and enjoy it is another matter. Especially since that mongrel Silvio took over Barbara's job after she opted for early retirement.' She gazed through the window unseeingly, despair in her tone. 'I honestly don't understand the selection process for some of these people. It's not as though there's a shortage of qualified applicants.'

Claire rested her arm on Briony's. 'I know. Despite the population growing, everyone's struggling to get decent employees. Even here in Featherwood Falls.'

Briony raised her eyebrows. 'Not a lot of employers to need them though, is there?'

'I dunno,' Claire said. 'Rhys and I go to the pub on a Friday night—to support old Ned more than anything —but we usually meet Ashley, Damien, Quinn, and Joanne for a drink or dinner. Our little town has grown since covid. You'll get a surprise. Quite a few new houses have been built, and some homes that belonged to older residents have been sold and renovated. Some farms have realigned their boundaries and sold chunks of land off too.'

'Wow. Featherwood Falls has moved with the times. What about the pub? It was looking pretty shabby the last time I was here.'

'It still does,' Claire continued. 'If road repairs are being done in the area, the guys have a drink there after work, and if the highway is busy or closed, tourists come this way instead. But Ned's pretty frail these days. He keeps on plodding and reckons he can't afford any more staff than he has—and that's pretty much only Ann, who does the cooking with a couple of teenagers who take turns to help her in the kitchen when Ned can afford it.'

'He still does all the bar work on his own?' Briony blinked with incredulity.

'Damian helps him if the pub gets really busy.' She snorted. 'But this is Featherwood Falls, not the Gold Coast.'

Briony mulled over the information while consuming two cups of coffee and several of the toasted cheese, ham, and tomato sandwiches.

As she chewed, she glanced at the family photo on the wall above the French doors, taken when the girls were in their early teens. Thoughts circled in her head as she studied the likeness between Claire and their father. For most of her life, people had said how much Briony resembled her mother—thick, wavy brown hair, curvy and shorter than her sister at fifteen, despite being two years older. While their hair colour and height differed, for the first time, Briony could see the family resemblance, reminding her of the weight loss that had left her face thinner and Claire-like.

She turned toward her sister, swallowing her mouthful. 'Do you think Ned would employ me?'

Both Ginny and Claire stared at her with surprise.

'I don't know that you would enjoy working there, love,' Ginny grumbled. 'The pub is not like those you've become used to. It's a bit run-down now, and Ned is not an easy man to work with.'

Claire twisted her mouth ruefully. 'True. He's a nice old guy but is deaf and won't do anything about it. Patrons have to shout at him to order, so it's sometimes an uncomfortable environment.'

Briony straightened, nibbling her lip. 'I won't get my hopes up, but maybe I could talk to him. Work out a plan that might appeal.' She met the questioning gazes of her mother and sister and sagged into the chair. Clearly, they knew more than she did—and were not hopeful. But if there was no employment here, what would she and Alex do—and where could they go? Panic surged in her chest.

'Come on. Get changed and we'll go for a ride and talk about things.' Claire rose and gathered the plates. 'Did you need us for anything this afternoon, Mum?'

'No. Kirk's fencing job at Kallala will take until dark, so I'll potter in the garden while you're gone. Take Bow and Echo with you. They haven't done any stock work for a few days and they're desperate for a good run.'

'How are they coming on?' Briony asked.

'Pretty good. Chime's past helping now, so I guess she's happy to let her children do the hard yards while she lies in the sun,' Ginny said, studying the old kelpie reclining on the veranda.

'We'll take Drum too. He's a great little dog and keeps those two rascals in line.' Claire laughed and slung an arm across her sister's shoulders. 'I'll bring the horses in while you change.'

Briony's heart leapt. It felt like eons since she'd been on a horse, and her muscles would protest initially. But, years earlier, she had been the more enthusiastic horsewoman of the two girls, and it was a skill and love she hoped she would never lose. This would be an excellent opportunity to test that theory.

4

———

Sam Frankham shoved the last item of clothing into his backpack as his heavy heart fought bitter thoughts. With a glance around the room, he shouldered the bag and headed to the reception area.

'Leaving us so soon?' The scantily dressed woman reached a delicate hand over the counter toward him, her bottle-blonde hair exposing a dark stripe against her skull. 'It's always the handsome ones who leave.'

A hot flush crept up Sam's neck at the woman's flirtatious insinuation. Swallowing the sarcastic comment that threatened to explode from his lips, he took a deep breath, propped his pack against his leg, and withdrew his wallet.

Peering behind him, the receptionist added, 'What

happened to your girlfriend? Had a tiff? Gave you the heave-ho?'

Sam stared at her unsmilingly, his jaw tight. He waved his card in front of her. 'If you'd process that payment for me, please, I'll be on my way.'

Her eyebrows lifted and she snorted. 'Like that is it? Gunna tell me where you're heading?'

He shrugged. 'No.' Privacy wasn't his reason for not sharing, even if she'd needed to know, which she didn't. He hadn't a clue where to go from here, and the urge to get away overrode his hatred of lies.

After sashaying to the card reader, she processed Sam's payment and handed him the receipt. 'Love to see you back any time,' she ended with an artificial grin.

After collecting his pack, he walked through the door to be greeted by a slap of icy air.

Slipping his arms through the straps, he hoisted the bag onto his back and lowered his head to fasten the clips as he strode forward.

'Where are you off to?'

The soft Irish accent instantly halted him. He turned to face Ciara King, the beautiful dark-haired woman he had fallen head over heels in love with a month earlier.

Blood pounded through his veins. 'I thought you'd gone for good ... ditched me.' He couldn't keep the bitterness from his voice.

'You silly man. Why would you think that? I told you I'd be a couple of days—and I'm only a little late.'

She reached up and pulled him to her. For a moment, he left his arms dangling, uncertain. Was this a dream—or a ploy for something he didn't know how to handle? Then, he wrapped her in an embrace, oblivious to the curious stares from passers-by. After several long seconds, he released her and placed his large, work-worn hands on her upper arms.

'In New Zealand, we consider a couple of days to be two—three at most. Australia's the same,' he said sternly. 'And ... if someone says they'll be back within that time and don't message or turn up, it usually means one of two things. Either something has happened to them ... an accident or worse. Or, they have changed their mind and have used the excuse to do a runner.' He paused, swallowing the unease from his voice. 'It's now four days since you left. You refuse to carry a phone, so I had no alternative but to ring the hospitals and police. They said your name hadn't been reported as a patient or in an accident, so I assumed you didn't want to see me again.

Her deep, sapphire-coloured eyes in her pretty heart-shaped face stared up at him, and he melted all over again—just as he had when they'd first met in the South Australia vineyard.

'I told you I had business to attend to in Melbourne and you were not to worry.'

He grunted, his initial relief at seeing her fading as the mysterious reason for her absence took over. 'Couldn't you have called me on a payphone? What did you expect me to think?'

Ignoring his questions, she hooked an arm through his and stepped forward. 'Come on. We don't need an audience and can talk later. You were heading for your ute—right?'

He nodded, his emotions wrestling inside his big, muscular body—a confusing jumble of love, relief, and embarrassment.

After working side by side in South Australia as they trawled their way up and down the rows of grapevines, her bright, vivacious manner had had him hooked. They had shared a room—and a bed—and when the harvest drew to its close, he had asked if she would like to travel with him.

She had jumped at the chance, declaring that with winter approaching, they should head north to Queensland and the Northern Territory. This brief stay in the outskirts of Melbourne had not been what Sam had expected but, revelling in the glow of early love, he had agreed to wait at the hostel until Ciara returned—"within a couple of days".

As a shower blew in from the south, he lengthened his stride and hurried to the underground car park where he had left his beloved Ford Ranger days earlier, with Ciara trotting at his side.

After piling their backpacks into the bed of the truck, Sam slid the cover closed and locked it as his stomach rumbled loudly with hunger.

Ciara reached up and kissed him before climbing into the vehicle. His heart did a flip.

'Not sure about you, but I'm starving. What about we get on the road out of here and stop at the first place we see that has good tucker?' he said.

'Sounds great.'

'What happened to the usual, "sounds grand" from the gorgeous Irish girl I said a temporary goodbye to four days ago?' His face softened, and he put the vehicle into reverse.

Shooting a glance at her as he backed out, shock reverberated through him. Her face had paled, her lips clamped tightly together as though fighting fury.

He braked for a second before continuing their exit, a puzzled frown fixing itself on his forehead. *What brought on that reaction? Saying she sounds more Australian than Irish?* Failing to understand the sudden change in her demeanour, he clenched his teeth and headed onto the highway.

'Did you go sightseeing while I was away?' she asked.

They had been driving for a full five minutes before she spoke, her question surprising him. What should he say? That he hadn't liked to explore any farther than what he could on foot in case Ciara returned and he missed being with her for one minute? That he had hung around the hostel, chatting with travellers coming and going and reading the pile of tattered books stacked in the shabby lounge? If he'd known she would be so long, he could have explored the sights and sounds of Melbourne—and perhaps visited his cousin who lived in the Macedon ranges. But he had obeyed her command to "stay here and don't leave" ... and waited for the girl he hoped would be the love of his life.

'No. I waited for you—until I couldn't wait any longer.'

'Sorry.' Her voice was small and soft, her lip quivering and her eyes filled with remorse.

His resolve shook tentatively and then melted. The Ciara he had fallen in love with had returned.

AN HOUR LATER, satisfied after an enormous meal of fish, chips, and salad at a roadside café, Sam reached a hand across the table and took hers. 'So ... are you ready to head off and soak up the sun? Or have you changed your mind?'

As though the conversation earlier had not taken place, she smiled again—that glorious wide beam that reached deep into his soul. 'Let's do it.' She paused for a moment. 'Only, I had to send some money to my family, so I'm not as flush as I was. Do you mind if we look for work as we go?'

'Of course not.' He tried not to frown at her unexpected question. They had received a good pay after finishing at the vineyard. While not a fortune, he'd predicted it would keep him going for two months or more, allowing him to see more of the country before having to look for another job. Pushing her unexplained absenteeism to the back of his mind, he straightened, determined to look at the positives.

They rose and returned to the ute hand in hand, swinging their arms while joyous laughter burbled from her.

'Any particular destination, madam?' he asked.

'Nope—let's just go north and stop wherever and whenever it feels right.'

Sam quirked an eyebrow at her, put the vehicle into gear, and planted his foot on the accelerator. In that second, all he wanted was to enjoy every second with this gorgeous young woman.

5

———

For three hours, Briony and Claire circumnavigated the paddocks, checking water troughs and fences as they rode and discussed work, relationships, travel, and finances. Except for the hectic weekend of Claire and Rhys's wedding six months earlier, it had been a year and a half since they had been together—mostly because of Briony's work demands. Although they spoke regularly on the phone, both agreed it was not the same as being together and enjoying an activity they adored, especially revisiting their favourite trails and haunts.

They had turned for home when Briony suggested they ride to the falls.

'It's a bit cold for a swim. Thought you were a beach baby now?' Claire grinned at her sister.

'I have no intention of swimming. I haven't

forgotten how icy that water is even in summer, but I want to take a look. Remember when Dad built the wall to increase the size of the pond? We thought we were so helpful, but now I think about it, we were small and were probably a pain in the butt.'

Laughing, Claire bent to unlatch the gate before they rode over the hill, following the narrow track they had traversed hundreds of times before.

Drawing near, Briony leaned her head back and sniffed the air like the dogs that trotted at their heels. 'You can't beat the scent of the bush, can you?'

'It's the best part of working here. I've got a great husband and a cosy little house in town, but having my office here means I'm back in my happy place and can walk or ride anywhere I like—when I'm not working, that is.'

'And when you ARE working.' Briony angled her head questioningly. 'Aren't you Mum's right-hand employee?'

'Of course. Maybe now you're home, I could take on a few more graphic art jobs and you can help Mum with the stock?'

Briony frowned. It was something she hadn't considered. But ... if Claire's suggestion came to fruition, there was still Alex. What would he do?

'Hey. Tell me more about this secret of yours. Or is it a project?' Briony asked.

'I said I wouldn't discuss it until we're with Mum

and Kirk.' Claire clamped her mouth shut, pressed her finger and thumb together, and drew them across her mouth as though zipping it shut.

'Okay. A hint then?'

'Let's just say Mum and Kirk are talking about their future and property—which may affect us both.'

Briony lifted an eyebrow. One hundred percent certain her mother would never leave Featherwood Station, she surmised the discussion could mean the ownership of the property might take a different turn. A wave of unease gripped her. Would they form a partnership? If they did, where would that leave her and Claire should something happen to their mother? The thought of the farm drifting out of the Shepherd family's hands didn't bear thinking about. She forced it from her mind and focused on the waterfall in front of her.

AFTER DISMOUNTING beside the gnarly red gum, they looped their reins over the hooks embedded in the knobbly lumps of bark. Then, having followed the dogs through the cluster of trees and bushes to the water's edge, Briony stood in silence, soaking up the music of the water cascading over the rocks and splashing into the pond. All around them, remnants of the ancient rainforest buzzed with insects while a frog croaked from a log beside the waterhole.

She stepped carefully over fallen branches and thick leaf litter before reaching out to touch the bark of the featherwood.

'Good old tree. Still standing after all that's happened. If only these trees could talk—they'd have some stories to tell, wouldn't they?'

Claire grunted. 'Yeah. Probably pretty gruesome tales, I reckon. About all their brothers and sisters being chopped down and turned into buildings—or furniture, or even firewood.'

Briony nodded in agreement, her thoughts drifting back to conversations with her father. It had broken his heart, knowing how much logging had occurred before he was old enough to control the issue. But when his grandfather died, he and his father had immediately stopped all clearing and gradually restored and replanted as compensation. Ginny and Kirk had followed Lyndon's plan, fencing out introduced pests from the property with kilometres of exclusion fencing and allowing every waterway and suitable paddock to return to native pasture and plant life, bringing back species unseen for decades.

Drum pressed his small, black and tan body against Claire, and the pups played in and around the water while Briony reflected on the information Claire had shared.

We are so lucky to have this. I will never let it go.

It was another fifteen minutes before they returned to the horses, mounted, and headed back to the homestead, riding in silence as the afternoon sun slid into the west, leaving a golden glow bathing the bush.

BRIONY BRUSHED Akela briskly before fastening the wool-lined rug around the mare's chest. A chilly wind had blown up in the last ten minutes, reminding her of her year on the Isle of Skye. After an eight-week tour of Europe, she had answered an advertisement for hotel staff in one of the graceful, historic hotels on the Sleat Peninsula. To her delight, her application had been successful, and she moved to the isle two days later. It had been her first night waitressing for a local wedding when she had met Alex, and their mutual attraction had been instant. Shared phone numbers had led to a date—hiking in the Cuillin Mountains, followed by dinner at a cute little restaurant in Portree.

When the pandemic paralysed the country, the tourism season and hotel custom came to a standstill, leaving Briony torn between the man she loved and the fearful panic that consumed her as the gateway to returning home slammed shut. In his usual gentle, understanding way, Alex had cleared the small flat behind his mother's café; removing stores and unnecessary junk that had accumulated over the years. Then the two of them had moved into it together.

'Ready, Claire?' Briony peered over Akela's back toward her sister, who was clipping the straps around the lanky Appaloosa's back legs.

'Yeah. I'll just get Splash an extra scoop of feed. He's such a good boy—but unlike Akela, this poor fella needs more than a biscuit of hay to keep the weight on him.'

After feeding and releasing the horses, the girls tended to the dogs before returning to the house.

'I can't wait to ring Alex. I don't want to wake the whole household, but I reckon he'll be up by now.'

'Is he staying in the café flat or at his parents' house?'

'At the house. He said they took turns with his parents, sister, and brother, spending two hours at a time sitting beside his grandfather before he passed away. It was nice that their beloved grandpa was never alone.' Briony swallowed the lump in her throat as Claire gave her a sympathetic smile.

'You miss him, don't you—Alex, I mean.'

'Of course I do. We've been together for over three years—longer than you and Rhys have known each other.' Conscious her tone was short, Briony rested a hand on Claire's arm. 'Sorry, I didn't mean to bite.'

'Hey, I get it. You're tired and stressed. Why don't you ring him, and I'll give Mum a hand with dinner.'

Briony shot Claire a grateful grin and took the steps two at a time. Calling a brief 'We're back' to Ginny, who was clattering saucepans in the kitchen, she headed to her bedroom.

RELIEVED WHEN ALEX answered after two rings, Briony slumped onto her bed, hoping they could share more than the previous brief calls had allowed.

'Can you talk?'

Alex gave a relieved chuckle. 'Yes—and I'm the only one in the house at the moment, so don't hold back.'

Briony wallowed in the love that flooded her despite the distance. 'So—how does it feel to be home again?'

'Different. Not only because of Grandpa, but ...' He paused for a few seconds. 'I know it's less than two years since I left, but everything seems smaller, greyer, and a lot colder than I remember.'

'Oh! I thought daffodils and crocus would be peeping through the ground.'

'Too early. The tulips are still flowering, and they brighten the place. But it's raining and miserable—and a long way from the Gold Coast.'

Briony murmured sympathy. 'Have you been anywhere or is everyone too sad to leave the house?'

His voice brightened. 'Yesterday Soph and I took Mum and Dad to Armadale for a drive. Visiting the woods was good for all of us.'

Briony recalled the vista of nodding blue heads that carpeted the ground throughout the Armadale woods each May. 'I love that place.'

'So did Mum. We wandered through there for a while, then went to the Ardvasar hotel for lunch. The wild garlic's flowering and there are hawthorn and rowan blossoms everywhere. You'd like it.'

Briony's mind drifted to the wildflowers that covered the hills and gullies on the isle, so different from the prickly pear and persistent boxthorn that plagued Queensland. Yellow marsh marigolds had brightened the damp ditches, adding to the green fields dotted with snowy-white sheep. Outside the home Alex grew up in was a small garden, but after a life amongst the vivid colours of Ginny's roses and salvias, to her, except for spring, it had seemed small and colourless.

Snapping from her momentary flashback, she asked, 'Is everything organised for the funeral?'

'Yes. Friends are bringing food to the wake, and Mum's been cooking while Dad's doing what he can at the café.' He chuckled again. 'You can imagine what the house smells like—no one will go home hungry after this funeral.'

'What about Hamish and Margie? How are they doing?'

'Margie's helping at the café when she can. Her mother looks after wee Chloe, and Hamish is doing his best to keep the boat running and bringing in enough fish to pay the bills. Once this is over, I suppose life will return to normal here.'

'What about your grandpa's croft?'

The Cunningham home was double the size of their grandfather's little stone cottage, but both dwellings contained the same familiar scents of furniture polish and the fragrance of food, whether from the old AGA in the cottage or baking in the modern oven that they had installed five years earlier. Aileen's talent for transforming any food item into something delicious and heartwarming ensured that the kitchen remained the heart of both dwellings.

Nostalgia washed over Briony for a few minutes as they chatted.

'I miss you, Briony, and I can't wait to be back in Australia again.'

'Me too,' she whispered, hugging her knees to her chest. 'How long do you think?'

'Not sure. The solicitor will talk to us about Grandpa's will after the funeral, then I can book my flight home. I'll ring after the lawyer has been.'

'Great. I'll be waiting.'

They paused for a moment before they both spoke in unison, saying, 'Love you,' and laughed.

6

$\mathcal{A}$lex and Sophie stood at the graveside, surrounded by family. Thick fog drifted over the town cemetery, enveloping them in its heavy, damp blanket.

Reaching out, Aileen clasped one of Sophie's and Alex's hands in each of hers, squeezing them gently. 'It's time to go home. Your grandpa would be proud of you both. You know what a stickler he was for loyalty to your employer, but he knew you were both with him at the end, even if he could no longer speak.'

Sophie choked back a sob and bent her head, brushing her face on the collar of her jacket. It hadn't been the reunion she had hoped for, but a small frisson of gratitude filtered through her.

She and Alex had reached home with twelve hours to spare before their much-loved grandfather passed away. It had been enough for them to sit beside the old man's bed and share their gratitude for the years he had patiently spent with his grandchildren, teaching them about the land, sea, and sky that surrounded the Scottish islands and the history that remained deep in their veins. Despite exhaustion taking its toll on them all, time allowed for their reassurance that the family would care for their homeland as previous generations had.

During their short stay, Sophie had listened to her brother's tales of Australia—the descriptions of beaches, smells, and the warm climate that a Scotsman would find hard to comprehend—while excitement quivered deep within her.

Alex didn't speak until they reached the hotel where the wake was taking place, functioning as though on auto as he acknowledged each familiar face and shook hands with those less well known. The room was warm and cosy; there was a fire blazing in the grate, and the crowd became jovial and nostalgic now the solemn part of the service was over and the alcohol flowed.

'Earth to Alex. Are you hearing me?' Sophie's gentle voice penetrated her brother's faraway gaze and he jumped.

'Sorry, Soph, I was thinking about Briony and wishing she were here.'

She linked her arm through his. 'I understand.

We're supposed to be mingling though—thanking attendees for coming, ensuring they've got a drink and a bite to eat, asking about their grandchildren and all that stuff.'

He apologised again before upending his glass and swallowing the last mouthful of whisky. Straightening, he disentangled his arm from Sophie's and they surged through the crowd to stand beside his parents while their father shared thanks and appreciation with friends, family, and strangers.

THE FOLLOWING DAY, with weary bodies and hovering headaches, the five Cunningham family members gathered in the cosy cottage that had been their grandparents' and home to generations of family before them. With its thick, stone walls and wide fireplace, it was no different to most on the island, with family photos decorating the dresser, hand-knitted rugs covering the back of the couch, and the smell of peat smoke drifting from the old fireplace dominating the room.

Malcolm McDonald—another Scot who had been born and raised on Skye and was both a solicitor and family friend—stood tall and solemn beside the hearth.

Clearing his throat, he passed each member a copy

of the will before he began reading. 'As you know, this is the last will and testament of Alexander Robert McKinnon, known to friends and family as "old Alex".' He paused and looked at Alex with the hint of a smile. 'Of course, that name stuck to him after your birth.'

Malcolm droned on while Sophie's mind drifted again to Alex's suggestion of her returning to Australia with him. She was sure Paul would allow her time off. But she wanted more. Not only to explore Australia, but other countries that had featured in her high-school studies—like Canada, the Pacific Islands, and Greece. A few weeks off wouldn't be enough. Perhaps she should resign—courteously, of course, and hope-fully with Paul's invitation to rejoin his team should she ever want to.

This time, it was she who needed an elbow nudge from Alex. She blinked and fixed her gaze on Malcolm.

'So, Aileen has been left with your grandfather's remaining savings and investments, including thirty breeding ewes and any lambs that remain on the croft, except for a sum of money bequeathed to you, Hamish, and Sophie. The cottage in which we now stand and the land attached to it belongs to Mr McKinnon's eldest grandson, Alex.'

Disbelief drew lines across Alex's face. 'But shouldn't Mum have got everything? As Grandpa's only child, I thought she would be his only beneficiary?'

Malcolm shrugged. 'It was not for me to tell your

grandfather what he should and shouldn't do with his property and possessions. This will was made five years ago, before you left for Australia.'

Alex met the variation of expressions on his parents' and siblings' faces. His mother smiled while his father nodded resolutely.

'Although you may be the owner of the McKinnon property, there's no law that says you have to live here,' said Bruce Cunningham. 'Neither your grandfather nor your mum or I would ever insist you stay when we know your heart is in Australia with Briony. There are other options—you may like to rent it out or turn it into one of those bed-and-breakfast places.'

'Or let us live in it,' Hamish said quietly.

Everyone turned to look at Hamish, who had sat mutely throughout the meeting.

'Margie and I haven't got enough for our own place yet, so instead of paying rent where we live now, we could pay you, Alex—and take good care of the place for future generations of our family.'

Before anyone else commented, Sophie chipped in. 'I think that's a good idea. I'm thinking of taking a year off to travel.' She turned to Alex. 'First stop, Queensland—that is, if Alex doesn't mind me tagging along. And when I come home, I doubt you'd mind me staying with you?' She swung her gaze to her parents.

'Of course not, love. We will welcome you anytime,' Aileen said softly, as though trying to process the unexpected suggestions. 'I didn't realise you were so keen to travel.'

'Dad?' Alex met his father's thoughtful stare. 'What do you think I should do with the cottage?'

'It's up to you, son. You know your mother and I are quite happy where we are—and we've got the café, flat, and the boat, so we are very comfortable. If you're content for Hamish and Margie to take care of the croft, I think it's a great idea.'

'So do I.' Alex spoke firmly, a finger and thumb on his chin as he contemplated his brother. 'I wouldn't expect you to pay rent either, Hamish. I think of the cottage as being part of this family—our family's heritage—and if you can maintain it, at least for a couple of years while Briony and I decide where we're going to make our home, I'll be happy.'

'Except you won't have any money,' Hamish said.

Alex paused for a second, then shrugged. 'I've got savings and can earn a lot more money in Australia than you can here. Think of it this way. I don't have to pay you a caretaker's wage and you don't have to pay me rent. So, we're square.'

Malcolm gave a small cough, as though asking for permission to speak. 'Can I suggest that, once you are sure about your choices, we draw up an agreement to that effect to prevent any disagreements that may arise in the future. Remember, you are all grieving at the moment and possibly still in shock. We don't always make good decisions in these situations.'

Sophie slumped on the couch and picked up Sebastian, the ancient tabby cat that had wandered his way into the sitting room through the partially open door. While he purred on her knee, she watched her brothers and parents continue the discussion with Malcolm, their quiet voices rising with excitement as solutions appeared to be made.

Their grandfather's inheritance through savings wasn't much—Malcolm suggested around six thousand pounds each to all except Alex after accounting for the fees and charges, but Sophie found it perfect for launching her travels. She could work as she went and besides, her bank account had been growing slowly but steadily, as though waiting for something to happen.

Stroking Sebastian with firm, caring hands, Sophie allowed a smile to creep over her face as excitement bubbled up inside her.

I'm off to Australia—and who knows where that will lead next.

7

Briony laid her knife and fork in the centre of her plate, casting her gaze around the four of them as her mother reached for Kirk's hand. Absent from the gathering, Rhys was conducting random drug and alcohol testing on the highway, so Claire had opted to stay for dinner and to hear the plans her mother had hinted at.

'While we're together, I want to discuss the farm with you,' Ginny began.

Briony waited, her gut churning with tension as a raft of possibilities swept through her.

'As you know, Kirk has his own house and farm, but spends most of his time here. So ... if it's okay with you girls, we would like him to move in permanently.'

Briony released the breath she had held with a whoosh. 'Is that all! Of course, Mum. This is your house and your farm, and Kirk's one of the family now.'

'Good grief, Mum. Is that all you're worried about?' Claire added, turning to rest a hand on Kirk's arm. 'If you promise to behave, we'll let you stay, mate.'

They laughed, a visible release of tension filling the room.

'That's not all.' Ginny drew a deep breath, removing her elbows from the table and clasping her hands in her lap. 'I'd like to make some changes to the ownership of Featherwood Station.'

Briony frowned while Claire stared at her mother.

'Like what?' Claire asked.

'Kirk will move in here, and I'll transfer the deeds of this property into our four names—a quarter to each of us. That way your future is secured, so even if you don't want to live here after I die, you will still own it no matter what happens. Of course, after I'm gone, my portion will become yours.'

An icy chill spread up Briony's back. 'Mum. Are you okay? Is there something you're worried about?'

Ginny grinned. 'There's nothing like that, love. It's just ... well, lately I've heard about a few locals who thought they had secured their farms for their family, but there was something hidden that only the deceased partner knew about—like a massive debt. Then they lost the lot.' She set her mouth in a firm line. 'I will not allow that to happen to us.'

'Good to hear,' Claire murmured.

'I want you both to know,' Kirk paused and took in a deep breath, speaking in a soft voice, his kindness shining through, 'I have no living children—you and your mother are my family. Ginny is also my partner, my love, and my best friend. As long as I live, I will protect her, work alongside her, and take care of her. But I do want us to live as a couple, and I assure you that when the time is right, or I pass on, my share in Featherwood Station will become yours.' He shared a wry smile. 'You never know, I might even convince your mother to marry me yet.'

Ginny stared at him, goggle-eyed. 'Is that a proposal?'

Without hesitation, Kirk pushed his chair back and lowered himself carefully onto one knee, gazing into her eyes. 'I guess it is. Ginny, will you marry me?'

With a delighted giggle, Ginny leapt up and reached for his hand, pulling him to his feet and hugging him tightly. 'Of course I will, you silly man. Now get up off those dodgy knees before you do yourself damage.'

As the four of them burst into a frenzy of congratulations, a fuzzy warmth filled Briony's veins. There was nothing she would like more than to see their beautiful mum have a second chance—permanently.

After the initial excitement, Kirk hushed them and continued, 'So, what I'm proposing, besides marrying your mother, is that my house and the acreage that goes with it become available for either or both of you to live in or buy if you prefer. Or … if neither of you want or need it at the moment, we could rent it out and invest the money in a joint project somewhere—maybe build more holiday cottages or something similar.' Although Kirk's sturdy frame supported hours of tedious manual labour, he had never been much of a talker and words clearly exhausted him.

Briony giggled at Kirk's ability to switch from the romantic marriage proposal to the practicality of his property. 'That's really kind of you, Kirk.' Her shoulders sagged. 'I wish I knew what Alex and I are going to do—but thank you for giving us an option.'

'Yeah. Me too. Rhys and I are happy living in the police house, but it would be nice to have something to call our own. After all, who knows if or when Rhys might decide he's had enough of being a police officer and want to go farming instead,' Claire finished. 'And now, I am going to crack open that bottle of Moët that's been in the fridge for months, waiting for a good reason to drink it.'

Following Kirk's example of practical conversation, Ginny said, 'We'll leave you both to talk things over with your partners, but meanwhile, I will be speaking to the solicitor about my will.'

'Are you sure there's nothing troubling you, Mum?' Briony spoke softly, her voice quavering with concern.

'No. I'm perfectly alright—except for getting old, which is a privilege your father didn't get. Good to know Featherwood Station will be in excellent hands for another generation or two, at least,' Ginny said.

Grinning at Claire, Briony added, 'That's you and me, girl. And I think she's hinting at grandchildren already.'

They laughed again, cleared the table, and opened the Moët.

BRIONY LEAPT out of the dining chair to snatch her phone off the bench, her heart beating with hopeful exhilaration at the ring tone—the special one that signalled it was Alex.

'Hi.' She flashed a grin toward the table where she had been enjoying the last of the Moët with Ginny, Kirk, and Claire. After mouthing, 'It's Alex. I'll go outside,' she wandered through the French door onto the veranda.

'Hey, darling. It's good to hear your voice.'

Her face softened at the strong Scottish accent. 'What's news?'

'I'm about to book my flight home—but I have a question for your mum.'

Briony waited. Why would he need to ask her mum anything? They all knew he was welcome at their homestead, and the family adored him. 'Okay-y. What is it?'

'Sophie wants to come to Australia. Do you reckon she could stay at the farm with us for a couple of weeks? She's fantastic with animals and you know she's a good worker.'

Briony laughed. 'Is that all? Of course she's welcome. We've got winter bookings for the farm-stay cabins, so she could give a hand there. We even have a couple booked who said they're coming to see the snow.' She snorted. 'Considering I've only seen it two or three times in my life here, we couldn't promise them anything, but the frost can get pretty hard, so hopefully that will do. I'm sure Mum will be grateful for help on the farm, especially as I'm keeping my fingers crossed for work at the pub for us.'

'Really? I thought it was a one-man hotel that barely survived with the population of Featherwood Falls.'

She pressed her palms together as though in prayer. 'Yeah, well. You never know. I'm hoping I can wheedle my way around old Ned and convince him we could make him a lot more money than he currently does.'

Briony shared the conversation about the farm and Kirk's property before Alex reciprocated, detailing the funeral and reading of the will.

'So it seems we're going to be property owners—

even if both situations come with slightly odd arrangements,' Briony said. 'How weird is that? This time yesterday, we owned nothing except the car and a heap of household goods. Now it looks like our lives are about to change—and this is a night of good news. Guess what?' Without waiting for his reply, she burst out, 'Kirk has asked Mum to marry him and, of course, she said yes. So, it looks like we're not the only ones planning a wedding.'

'That's fabulous news.' Alex chuckled softly. 'Please pass on my congratulations. I'll tell Sophie we can book our flights now and you let me know how you get on with Ned.'

'I will. Send me the details and I'll be there to meet you.'

They finished their call, and Briony stepped out of the icy wind and back into the warmth of the living room.

Kirk met her hopeful grin.

'Alright?' he asked.

'Alex says congratulations. It's okay if Alex brings his sister back with him, isn't it?'

Kirk nodded, and Ginny stared at her as if she had two heads. 'Of course. She's one of the extended family.'

Ginny stood, her head angled, her voice rising with hope. 'There's plenty to do, and Claire said she's got a few extra projects happening, so probably won't have as much time to help with the stock work. Perhaps Sophie can help me, that is if you and Alex find a job somewhere else?'

Briony's innards squeezed. The last thing she wanted to do was to put extra pressure on Kirk and her mother. 'How about we have dinner at the pub tomorrow?' she said. 'That way we can celebrate your good news, and I can see how busy it is and how Ann is coping with cooking meals.' She cast a hopeful glance at her mother.

'Sounds nice.' Ginny looked at Kirk. 'Okay with you? Or shall we ditch the girls and do it alone?'

He shrugged. 'I haven't got any urgent work on tomorrow. We'll slip into Warwick first and have a look at rings before you change your mind.'

'I won't change my mind about marrying you—and Briony, of course we'd love to join you, Claire, and Rhys for dinner. It's only Tuesday, so the pub won't have a busy schedule—unless poor old Ned loses his marbles, of course.

Briony chuckled.

The huge, mountain man who had won all the Shepherd girls' hearts had a twinkle in his eye as he stroked his grey-streaked beard. 'I hope you like stew.'

'I'll ring Ann in the morning and ensure there is at least one alternative.' Claire rose to her feet and moved to the kitchen with a pile of dirty dishes. 'Wait 'til I tell Rhys the news.'

8

When Kirk opened the door into the bar of the Featherwood Falls Hotel, Briony was relieved to see five men perched on high stools around a table by the window and another couple deep in conversation in the corner. Ned had his back to the entrance while voices drifted through the adjoining door between the bar and the dining room.

'Phew. We're not the only ones here,' Briony muttered.

They approached the bar, Briony standing back with Ginny, Rhys and Claire while Kirk leaned on the solid wooden bench and waited for Ned to turn and greet them.

When he didn't, Kirk cleared his throat noisily. Nothing.

'Gidday, Ned,' he said in a deep, booming voice.

The little man appeared engrossed in the football game on the television screen, and he turned with a start, bumping his hip on shelving running along the wall behind the bar. Unaware of the clattering glassware behind him, he peered through rheumy eyes at Kirk. 'Hello, young fellow. Didn't hear you come in. What'll it be?'

Kirk ordered a lemon, lime, and bitters for Briony and Claire, a glass of wine for Ginny, and a beer each for Rhys and himself.

The five of them exchanged wide-eyed glances as Ned proceeded to prepare the drinks with shaking hands. When he filled Briony's glass with lemonade, omitting the lime and bitters, Briony glared at her mother.

Eventually, carrying drinks that they'd accepted despite not being what they ordered, they retreated to a small table, putting enough distance between them and the other patrons to prevent any overheard conversation.

'Mum. He's terrible!' Briony whispered furiously. 'He looks like he's about to collapse. Surely, he can't expect to continue running this place.'

Ginny grimaced and leaned forward. 'I admit I haven't been in for months and didn't realise how much he had failed. I wonder if Lola and Frank have seen him lately.'

Their discussion continued for a few moments

before they moved into the dining room to order dinner.

Almost immediately after sitting down, a middle-aged woman with a red face approached, wiping her hands on a small towel. 'Hello, folks. How are you?'

'Hi, Ann.' Ginny reached for the handwritten card on the table, indicating the evening choices. 'What do you recommend?'

'The beef hotpot is popular. Or the fish and chips. Truck came through today, so the fish is fresh—well, as fresh as we can expect when we don't live by the sea. What'll it be?'

Ginny glanced at each of her companions. At their nods, she ordered fish and chips for everyone.

'Got it. Won't be long,' Ann said and hurried toward the kitchen.

Briony gazed around the room. The only other diners were a middle-aged couple who stood, collected their coats from the back of their chairs, and moved toward the counter to pay their bill. Although she accepted some of the bar patrons had possibly ordered a meal, she was miffed at Ann's reason for seeming flustered—almost curt. She didn't know the woman, but everyone in town had heard about the days she had cooked for a shearing team before moving to Featherwood Falls. Gossip had it that Ned had pressured her to help in the kitchen, but over the years, her cooking duties had grown to include doing her best to keep the pub clean, tidy, and open. Now Briony wondered if her dishevelled appearance resulted from being overworked—and probably underpaid.

Surprisingly, when the meals arrived, they were enough to feed a large man who hadn't eaten for days.

Briony speared a chip with her fork and turned it over to inspect it 'Wow. This fish is delicious, and the chips are cooked to perfection. Salad is fresh and crisp too.' Inclining her head toward the kitchen, she leaned closer to her mother. 'I think it's Ann who's keeping this pub alive, not Ned?'

Ginny continued eating, her eyes narrowing as a crash sounded from the bar. Footsteps thumped together with audibly anxious voices, triggering Kirk and Rhys to push their chairs back while Briony sat motionless, her fork poised in midair.

'I'll check on Ned.' Kirk's long strides had him at the adjoining door in a flash.

Rhys and the women followed him as Ann hurried from the kitchen.

After tucking her forearms under the old man's armpits, she hoisted him to his feet. 'It's okay. Ned's just taken a little tumble,' she said reassuringly.

Brushing a frail, blue-veined hand over his face, Ned coughed and muttered, his voice little more than a croaky whisper. 'I'm alright. Just a trip.' His attempt at a grin was more like an old theatre curtain rising, leaving regular wrinkles in the fabric. The sighs of relief from the patrons were audible.

'It's those ridiculous slippers of yours, isn't it, Ned?' Ann chided, staring at the old man's feet. 'I've told you before, they're not suitable for bar work. Rhys has spoken to you about wearing proper enclosed shoes, and if a cop from out of town was to do a random compliance audit, you'd be in trouble. More trouble than you are in now, anyway.' She shook her head as she moved away, muttering, 'Silly old fool.'

Without a word, the five of them returned to the dining room and finished their meal as they quietly discussed the problem.

'It would be awful if the pub was closed down.' Briony studied the beautiful timber walls and carved fretwork above the doors. 'There's a lot of history here, and if Ned doesn't hand over the reins and let someone get on with maintenance, the place is at risk of being closed, whether he likes it or not.'

'I'm having morning tea with Lola and Frank tomorrow. They're dying to see you again and hoped you'd come with me, Briony,' Ginny said with a wry twist of her lips. 'I thought I'd better get in before the gossip starts about Kirk and my engagement. Ned has a lot of respect for them both and if we suggest they have a chat with him, perhaps he will get off his high horse and think about what changes he needs to make.'

Kirk grunted. 'Changes. He needs to sell the place.

Let someone else breathe some money and life into the place. If I was twenty years younger, I'd consider it myself.'

They stared at each other in silence, no one voicing their thoughts, least of all Briony. *It's too soon and I can't get my hopes up.* But ... could this be the project they shared?

Too full to consider dessert, they called out their thanks to Ann, paid their bill, and retreated to the car. As Claire and Rhys walked along the footpath to the police station, Briony slid into the back seat of her mother's car, her pulse pounding while ideas flung around inside her head at the speed of a washing machine.

What if she and Alex could buy the pub? What would it be worth? Despite Kirk's suggestion they could join forces in a new project, she was certain that owning a run-down hotel would be something she and Alex might afford without requiring financial backing from anyone other than the bank.

Her veins fizzed with excitement, her spirits rising. She would discuss the possibilities with Alex after she'd crunched some figures and her mother had talked to Lola and Frank. Would he be prepared to settle in Featherwood Falls? She recalled the phone conversation they'd had the previous night. Although she understood Alex's grandfather would ensure the croft remained in the family, a tiny piece of her had thought her fiancé might have inherited something to help boost their nest egg—like in so many of the romance books she enjoyed.

But new hope surfaced. With the Scottish croft in Alex's name, and her quarter share in Featherwood Station, they had assets, even if their bank balances weren't huge. She was certain the bank would loan them all they'd need. Then, the Featherwood Falls Hotel would rise from its well-worn floorboards and they could begin a whole new life.

9

S am slammed the door and stared through the windscreen. 'Where do you want to go?' He kept his gaze on the creek below them, preferring the sight of gently trickling water as it flowed through the vegetation to Ciara's angry face.

'Who cares? Anywhere,' she answered, her voice bitter and despondent.

He shrugged, annoyance creeping through him. He had been enjoying the coast—and the Coffs Harbour area. The ocean, the vibe, and the casual lifestyle had grown on him over the previous ten days. He'd almost thought they could find work in the town and stay for the winter. But no. Ciara was different. A departure from the free, wild spirit he had fallen in love with, she had become sullen and bad-tempered.

He reflected on when it had begun. Had her

sudden change somehow been his fault? His memory drifted back two days when a couple had stopped to talk to her as she sat on the sand, reading. He had been treading water, deciding whether he should wait until another wave arrived that he could body surf to the shore or call it quits and head in for lunch. While his belly rumbled, Ciara had been partially hidden by the couple, so he'd focused on the waves and caught a big one that carried him within metres of her. The man and woman had gone—and Ciara was fuming but refused to talk. Her tight-lipped anxiety had continued for hours, her over-the-shoulder-glances frequent as though checking to see no one was following.

'Are you worried about something?' he'd asked after arriving back at the camp.

She unzipped the tent and flung herself face down on the air bed. 'Of course not.'

He flinched at her curt retort. 'Who were those people you were talking to on the beach the other day? Did they upset you?'

'They thought I was someone else—someone they'd met in London, but they were wrong.'

'Okay.' He paused for a few moments before saying cautiously, 'I like it here and thought we could stay and look for work. What do you think?'

'I'm tired of this place. It's time to move on.'

He studied her mutely, breathing his anxiety away

while deciding whether he should leave her or kiss her.

'Don't even think about it,' she snapped.

He bristled at her venom, any hint of intimacy quickly vanishing. If that's what she wanted, it was fine by him. He had only one year to see all he could. Then he would either return to New Zealand and his family's company where he would work alongside his father—creating beautiful kitchens and bookcases for all and sundry—or make a new life somewhere else and relinquish the position his parents had agreed to hold for him.

Musing over his options, he jumped as she sat up suddenly.

'Let's head inland. We can pick up fresh food in Bellingen, then move to the New England area for a couple of weeks before it gets any colder.'

'Okay.' A frown crept over his forehead as she began stuffing clothes into her rucksack. *What happened to chasing the sun?* 'Do you mean we go now?'

She glared at him. 'Yes. Now.'

He blinked rapidly. What had caused this sudden decision? Recalling their conversation as they had neared Melbourne after grape-picking, he clamped his mouth shut. Her announcement—more like an order—that he stay in the hostel while she sorted out personal issues in the city had upset him but, desperate to keep the peace ... and the relationship, he had obeyed. This time, at least they would be together. And wherever they stayed, as long as she was with him, he convinced himself he was content and that her current moodiness was both temporary and forgivable.

TWO HOURS LATER, they approached Bellingen. Relieved that Ciara was back to her usual bright and cheerful self, Sam relaxed.

Mist drifted through the town, and as they left, a warning in Coffs Harbour advised of a southerly change that would bring heavy showers and storms over the central and coastal New South Wales region for the next week, along with significantly colder temperatures.

'Perhaps we should look for somewhere warmer and more weatherproof than the tent tonight,' he said.

Ciara shook her head. 'Don't be silly. This won't be any different from a normal Irish summer day.'

Later that night, huddled in their sleeping bags as rain lashed the flimsy tent and Sam felt sick with worry, Ciara slept soundly.

Dorrigo had seemed the perfect place to stop for a while—pretty, filled with birdlife and beautiful scenery, Ciara had declared it was ideal and directed him to the Dangar Falls camping area north of the town.

Something inside Sam shifted as he lay there, listening to the rain and the sound of the waterfall crashing over rocks. It was peaceful, and Ciara's eyes had sparkled as she'd planned days of bushwalking and places to visit while poring over the brochures Sam had gathered from the campground office. He hoped it would last.

The knot that had wedged itself in Sam's stomach earlier in the day, unravelled. Whatever or whoever had upset Ciara seemed to be behind them now and he could rest easy—for a while, anyway.

10

———————

 riony leaned on the car, her mind a tangle of questions as she tapped the roof with impatient fingers and gazed over the valley. It was a glorious autumn day, with clear blue sky and enough bite in the air to remind her that winter wasn't far away. When Ginny finally slid into the passenger seat with a container of scones on her lap, Briony let out a relieved breath and switched on the engine.

Hours spent on her laptop the previous evening had been both fruitful and depressing. Briony had delved into real-estate values, recent sale prices of country hotels, accommodation places of all sorts, and the current costs of historic-building renovations. Finally, she had drawn up a spreadsheet to compare loan rates, reported sales, and values in the Darling

Downs area. The result wasn't as positive as she had hoped, but it wasn't out of the question either.

The next step for her was to see if Lola and Frank would be successful in encouraging Ned to sell the hotel—and if that didn't succeed, at least in employing both her and Alex. She reasoned that way all would not be lost. It would give them a chance to gauge the clientele and have a good look at maintenance requirements at the same time.

Satisfied with her homework, she only needed the upcoming conversation with Lola and Frank to occur before she could email Alex all the details.

It HAD BEEN months since Lola's heart surgery, and although she had returned to her jovial, kind self, there was a frailness about her that Briony had not seen before but knew better than to display concern.

'You look great!' Briony lied as Lola wrapped her in a warm embrace, her rainbow earrings tickling her cheek as she pressed against the older woman's ample chest.

Lola held Briony at arm's length and frowned. 'And you look too skinny.'

Briony shrugged as Frank took his turn to hug her. 'Don't worry about her, love. You know she's tried to fatten me up for decades—and it hasn't worked.' He grinned and swept his hands down his thin, wiry body.

'I'll put the kettle on,' Ginny said as she made her way to the kitchen, pointing at the basket beside the couch. 'Another baby, Lola?'

'Yes.' Lola shrugged. 'I can't help it. Said I wouldn't raise any more now our little grandson is on his way.' She reached into the blanket cocooning a tiny eastern grey joey. 'But you know me. I thought this little one might bond with the baby when he arrives, and they can grow up together.'

Ginny chuckled. The baby would be their second grandchild after Zoe, the granddaughter they hadn't known existed until a few months earlier. Her arrival had changed their world and even more so, the lives of both their only son, Ryan, and Emma, the local school-teacher's aide, bringing them together again after twenty-five years. The result of which had been renewed love, a quiet wedding with immediate family, and the joys of pregnancy with the baby due in September.

Briony fiddled with her hair, swallowing her coffee too quickly and burning her mouth in her haste to get on with the subject she was waiting for most—Ned. Eventually, she perched forward on her chair when Ginny brought up the subject of their pub dinner the previous evening.

'Ned had a fall.'

Lola clutched at her chest and tut-tutted. 'I've been worried about him for a while. Is he alright?'

Ginny nodded. 'Yes. He was wearing old slippers and being so frail, he must have turned too quickly. His foot came out of the slipper and he fell. No bruises that we could see, and he said he was fine.'

'Oh dear. I don't see him much of course—but Frank pops in every few days and keeps me posted.'

They all laughed at her unintended pun. As the operators of the general store and post office for almost forty years, the post was one of Frank's biggest responsibilities—and knowing what the residents of the small town were doing and if anyone was in ill health was part and parcel of Lola's daily conversations.

'Has he said anything about retiring? Or selling the pub?' Ginny asked.

Lola shrugged. 'A few locals have been on at him about that lately. If he doesn't decide soon, the pub will fall down around him—or he will drop dead behind the bar!'

Her exclamation startled Briony. She certainly didn't wish the old man dead, but if he could be talked into retiring ... A frisson of hope bloomed.

'I was wondering if he might employ Alex and me. Alex is an excellent chef and I'm sure I could run the bar—and get that area out the back tidied up so patrons could sit there and enjoy the view over the creek.'

Both Lola and Frank stared at her wide-eyed.

'Are you saying you and Alex want to run the pub?' Lola said.

'Well, yes. Maybe even own it one day.' Briony hesitated. 'We've been saving hard and have a big enough deposit to buy something of our own. I guess we were thinking more of a café like Alex's mother owns in Scotland, but with the state both Ned and the pub are in, I'm thinking a rescue project here in Featherwood Falls would be more appropriate for us.'

Having not shared her thoughts with her mother until she had done her due diligence, Briony now had everyone's attention.

'Briony! That's a wonderful idea.' A frown formed on Ginny's forehead. 'There will be costs involved in restoring it to its former glory, but Kirk's a builder and we're all pretty handy with a paintbrush and hammer.' Her eyes glazed over as a soft smile replaced the frown. 'This could be the family project we talked about.'

Lola shuffled forward in her chair and placed her empty cup on the table. 'I think your idea's an excellent one, Briony. With the experience and talents you and Alex have gained, you could grow the business—turn the dining room and menu into a place everyone wants to go and eat. Not only the locals, but people from out of town too. Maybe weekend lunches and family nights could become a "thing" ... Oh, the possibilities are endless.'

'And if you're worried Lola might think you're taking some of her business, don't be,' Frank said, crossing his arms over his chest. 'She needs to slow down, and if we had another food outlet in town we could recommend to passers-by, she wouldn't feel the pressure to keep up with the cooking here.'

'That's true,' Lola agreed. 'I could keep making my lamingtons and pies and serve coffee and tea. I'm sure that wouldn't affect the pub trade. Actually, having the two businesses running would probably help both of us.'

'We could do most of the renovations, even if we have to sub-contract a few jobs. No harm in asking, is there?' Briony said, desperately trying to keep a lid on her soaring hopes in case they came to nothing.

Ginny pressed a finger against her jaw as she responded. 'True. But let's not get ahead of ourselves yet. It's clear we all think it's a great idea, but we're missing one fact. Will Ned?'

'It's time he gave more consideration to his patrons, as well as himself.' Lola's brisk tone gave Briony confidence and her hopes rose even more.

'Right then.' Lola rose and began collecting the empty plates. 'While you two go home and discuss the pros and cons of renovating the old place with Kirk, Frank and I'll wander down to the pub and have a chat with Ned. Janet's in the shop this morning and Ryan will be back from the mail run shortly—and I doubt the pub will be busy yet.' She glanced up at the wall clock and pursed her lips. 'Actually, we've got less than an hour before the lunchtime drinkers drift in—so, come on, Frank, get your skates on.'

At that moment, Ginny wrapped her left hand around her mug as she stood.

Lola sucked in a noisy, delighted breath. 'Ginny! Is that what I think it is?'

Ginny ducked her head coyly. 'Yes. I wanted to tell you Kirk and I are getting married.'

Lola flew at her, almost knocking the mug out of her hand in an exuberant hug. 'How wonderful!' she almost squealed. 'What a gorgeous ring.'

Pink heat crept up Ginny's neck onto her cheeks as Lola peered at the pair of exquisite diamonds entwined with tiny, engraved leaves on the gold band. 'It belonged to Kirk's grandmother,' Ginny said. 'He wanted to buy me one but, when he showed me this, we decided it was more meaningful as well as more beautiful than anything I could ever want. It needs adjusting and a good clean, so we'll get that done. I really only wore it today to show you—and to see how observant you are.'

While they laughed and Ginny divulged more details to her insatiable friend, Briony gathered up the remaining dishes and delivered them to the sink. As she dismissed Lola's excitement over her mother and Kirk's good news, her mind raced ahead with plans for the hotel. What had been a mere passing thought less than twenty-four hours earlier had now become a possibility—a strong one.

THE MINUTE BRIONY and Ginny entered the homestead, Briony nipped into her room and opened her laptop. As she'd hoped, an email had arrived from Alex with flight details and, as she scanned it, her head spun with anticipation.

Waiting for what she prayed was a positive call from Lola—and for the hours to pass before Alex would be awake and they could talk coherently—was torture. Briony tried practicing deep breathing, to no avail. A distraction was required.

Claire jumped as Briony appeared in the doorway. 'I'm going for a ride before lunch. If I saddle the horses, will you come?'

Clearly distracted by the array of papers spread over her desk, Claire tilted her head for a second. 'Sure. I've got about five minutes left on this job then was going to have a break. A ride sounds great—stretch a few muscles before I get back into it.'

'Done.' Briony sped out of the house, pulling on riding boots and a jacket before jogging toward the stables.

Four days. She had four days to discuss the

purchase—or otherwise—with Alex, put a business plan together, confront Ned with an offer if Alex was agreeable, and be in Brisbane to collect both Alex and Sophie.

She just needed Ned's approval.

11

After a gentle canter across the paddock, they slowed to a walk, and Briony shared her thoughts and dreams with her sister.

'Fantastic idea—if Ned's agreeable,' Claire said cautiously. 'And Alex, of course.'

Briony's shoulders straightened. 'I know. I've thought about that, but I have a good feeling. We talked of a joint project the other evening, but I think I would rather we owned the pub ourselves. If I am a part-owner of this farm, and Alex is the owner of a Scottish croft—even though he didn't inherit any money—our borrowing capacity should be stronger, shouldn't it? We've been saving like crazy too, so have a good deposit stashed away. Now the only thing we need is for Ned to agree.'

'Yep—and convince the bank, of course.'

They were silent for a few minutes as thoughts swarmed like a hive of bees in Briony's head.

'What did Rhys say about Kirk's house?' The random question popped into Briony's mind, and she squirmed with guilt. Her whole being had been consumed with ideas for herself and Alex, and she'd given no further thought to how Claire felt about the family discussion.

'Rhys doesn't make decisions quickly. But the more we think about it, the more we like the idea of buying Kirk out, even if we continue living in the police house for a while and put tenants in the house.'

'Good plan. So … if everything works out the way we hope, we could both be property rich and flat broke within weeks.'

They burst into laughter as they approached the stables.

BEFORE THEY REACHED THE GATE, Ginny appeared, running across the paddock waving wildly.

'He said yes!' she yelled.

Briony's eyebrows shot up as she leapt off Akela. 'You mean Ned?'

'Yes.' Ginny leaned against Akela's neck, panting. 'Lola rang. Said to tell you Ned had another fall this morning, despite changing his slippers for enclosed shoes. So, when she and Frank expressed their concern and suggested he consider selling the pub, he fumed. Said he wasn't ready to retire. But they had a cup of coffee with him while Ann managed the bar. He eventually admitted he hasn't been feeling very well but doesn't want to sell his precious pub to some out-of-towner. Nor does he want to leave Featherwood Falls. Lola asked him how he would feel if a local was to take it over.' Her voice rose with excitement as she breathlessly finished relaying the information. 'He refused to discuss it at first, but they pointed out the advantages and calmed him down, and he became more interested. She asked him if he would be prepared to talk to you about it and he agreed!'

'Fantastic!' Briony hugged her mother tightly. 'I can't wait to tell Alex now—and get things moving.'

Pressing her head into Akela's side, she undid the girth and removed the saddle before turning to face her mother again.

'What does Kirk think about the state of the building? You mentioned that a few improvements had been made in the couple of years before Ned's wife died. Does that mean it's structurally sound and has passed council inspections?'

'I don't know, love. Let's pop down together and talk to Ned somewhere quietly, and we can have a thorough look through the upstairs and out the back while we're there. Before you launch into buying it, you need to have a clear knowledge of what's needed. I'll ring Lola and tell her we'll pick her up on our way. I'm sure Ned will be more agreeable if she's with us.'

Briony nodded before brushing Akela briskly while Claire took care of Splash.

'I'll let these two go while you and Mum get ready. I've got a job to finish, otherwise I'd come too,' Claire said.

A mixture of anticipation and fear bubbled up inside Briony. Although she had known that one day she and Alex would own their own business, the thought of becoming publicans in the historic hotel in her own hometown had never crossed her mind. It was more than she could imagine, but deep down, provided they could afford it, the prospect was perfect.

THEY WERE ALMOST at the store when Ginny said quietly, 'I want you to know that Kirk and I have discussed this possibility and are prepared to back you as guarantor on any loan if it's needed.'

Tears pricked Briony's eyes as she reached out to touch her mother's arm. 'Thank you, Mum. That means the world to me—but I'm hoping it won't come to that.'

Ten minutes later, while Kirk conducted a thorough assessment of the building, Briony and Ginny sat in the corner of the dining room with Lola and Ned.

'Lola told me you're interested in this pub.' Ned's voice filled with anxiety.

'Yes. I believe you are thinking of retiring.'

'Well. I don't want to. But I'll admit it's getting too much for me now. What are you planning?'

'We are looking to buy a business and had thought about a café. However, since coming home, I've realised how wonderful it would be if, presuming you retire soon and you find somewhere nice to live, we could have first offer on the hotel—if you decide to sell it,' Briony finished hopefully.

He studied her thoughtfully before turning to Lola. 'It's what you and Frank want me to do, isn't it?'

Lola nodded. 'We worry about you, Ned. None of us are getting any younger. The stairs are difficult for you now and we want you to be safe and happy.'

Ned heaved a reluctant groan. 'I s'pose.'

'Perhaps Lola could help you,' Ginny said. 'She knows the district nurses and has quite a bit to do with the council, what with her animal rescue and her shop. Have you thought about the council cottages?'

Lola took a deep breath. 'I heard Fred Brooks has been transferred to the hospice. Not looking good for him,' she said. 'He won't be returning to his cottage, and I thought perhaps we should make enquiries there if you're agreeable.'

He narrowed rheumy eyes and sat in contemplative silence for what seemed like long minutes. 'Do you reckon they might consider me for his cottage? I've visited him a few times. We were old mates when we were younger. I reckon I'd be happy there, and I'll consider anything if I don't have to leave Featherwood Falls and my friends.' His face hung in such sad folds, a lump of guilt formed in Briony's chest.

Years earlier, a row of tiny dwellings had been constructed on a lane parallel to the main road. Maintained by the local authority and visited daily by the district nurse, the cottages were provided to aging and needy locals under a reduced rental agreement.

Ned brightened, straightened his back, and shuffled in his chair. 'I s'pose I could be talked into having this hotel operated by a local if I could trust them not to sell it to some townie.' The old man's voice wavered with frailty.

Empathy filled Briony. After living in the hotel his entire life, she understood why Ned would not want to leave the village. *Probably why he has refused to think about it.*

Briony leaned forward. 'You know my family well, and although you've only met Alex once when we were here for Claire and Rhys's wedding, we would like to make this lovely establishment our home and business, if we can.'

· · ·

WITH FINGERS CROSSED as she rested her hands in her lap, she reassured him there was no hurry.

'We won't know until we ask about the cottage,' Lola said. 'I'll get on to them as soon as I get home. Are you happy with that, Ned?'

Satisfied an alternative for Ned might be in the offing, Briony cleared her throat. 'Would you be prepared to sell the hotel to us if you could continue living in Featherwood Falls?'

'I might be. I'm not out to make squillions, but we need to agree on a fair price—and sort out the transfer of the liquor licence.'

'Of course. Will the licence transfer take long?'

'I'll get on to Liquor Licencing and find out what has to be done to transfer it to you and Alex.'

At Ned's sudden change of attitude, Briony's hopes soared.

It's a done deal! She wanted to shout.

'It could take a few weeks—and I'll need to decide on the sale price. If you're genuinely interested, perhaps you and Alex could manage the place until we sort out an agreeable sale? That way, while we wait until I find somewhere to live, you can get the feel of what it's like to run a hotel.' He stroked his tatty beard before continuing. 'I assume you've both got your RSA certificates—you know, the Responsible Service of

Alcohol qualification? Bloody thing,' he muttered as his concentration appeared to wander. 'Made me do it years ago—despite having served here for nigh on sixty years at the time.'

'Yes. We have. We've both worked in hospitality—and managed various businesses for a few years now,' Briony said, desperate to keep Ned's attention on the potential exchange.

Kirk entered the room at that moment, a relieved grin on his face. He passed his notebook to Briony and ran through his notes.

'Find anything nasty?' Ned asked.

Kirk shook his head. 'Not really. Structurally, things look okay. It appears this building was constructed from good, native hardwood and miraculously seems to have been untouched by termites except in the room at the back of the building. Is that a bedroom, Ned?'

'Yeah. It was the room me and my wife used for decades. After she died, I couldn't bear to be there on my own, so I moved across the hall into the room we'd been using for storage. It was mine when I was a kid.'

Again, a wave of compassion ran through Briony while part of her silently apologised for being the one to change the old man's life.

'The floor will need replacing ... and potentially some of the wall frame,' Kirk added. 'But the main beams appear unaffected. Looks like the termites were treated and haven't returned, so you're very lucky. I'll get Geoff to double-check everything though in case I've missed something.'

'Who's Geoff?' Briony asked.

'A building inspector. Lives in Warwick, and we've had a bit to do with each other over the last couple of years. He did a thorough check of the buildings at Kallala before I started working there.'

'Okay.' Briony glanced at the list again. 'The roof?'

'Hmm. It's got a bit of rust, but I reckon replacing a few sheets of iron in the worst spots will ensure it's watertight for another few years. The repair and restoration costs will be manageable, and I promise I won't charge much.' He chortled, and Ginny slapped him lightly on the arm.

'What he means is that we are both providing our labour for free. As family, it's the least we can do, especially if we can restore this lovely place to its former glory.'

Creases around Ned's eyes deepened as the hint of a smile spread. Clearly buoyed by the building report —and the possibility of somewhere to move to—he retreated to the bar before returning with a pen and paper. Then, in black, spidery script, he gave Alex and Briony written authorization to join his meagre work-force until the settlement date arrived. 'Just in case something happens to me before we get this all sorted out, you have my word in writing. I'll ring the solicitor and have a talk with him tomorrow.'

Briony felt as though she might explode with happiness.

THE DISCUSSION with Alex later that evening further boosted Briony's optimism.

'I've got an appointment with the bank in the morning and I'm hoping any paperwork we need to sign will be ready by the time I've collected you from the airport. We can stop off on the way home and get that ball rolling, provided Ned has done his part.'

'Sounds like you've thought of everything.' Joyful appreciation and a touch of wonder was reflected in his tone.

They talked for another fifteen minutes before confirming flight times and saying goodbye.

Then, lying back on her bed, surrounded by spreadsheets and sticky notes, Briony rested her hands on her ribcage and stared through the window. Stars dotted the charcoal sky and from somewhere outside, the familiar hoot of a Boobook owl sent a friendly signal. Everything would work out for the best. She just had to wait.

12

By the time Briony was driving out of Brisbane with Alex beside her and Sophie in the back seat, her excitement had overflowed and her companions were as enthusiastic as she was.

'Perhaps you'll be able to employ me?' Sophie suggested.

'Maybe—if you're prepared to work for free accommodation and food,' Briony laughed. 'Mum's got plenty of jobs lined up for you on the farm, but I'm sure between getting the pub shipshape and the yard out the back cleaned up and turned into an outdoor beer garden, none of us will be bored. Alex will be introducing more menu items, and we'll plan a few special events to bring in more custom as soon as it looks better.'

'We should have a big opening—invite the whole

town. Put a spit roast on and celebrate the rebirth of the Featherwood Falls Hotel,' Alex said jovially.

Briony slapped his arm. 'You haven't even seen it yet ... well, except for the time you came with me before Claire and Rhys's wedding. We've only ever had one drink there.'

'True. We'll remedy that this afternoon.'

DELIGHTED WITH NED'S change of heart and his decision to hand the pub over as soon as possible, even if they were only going to be managing the place initially, Briony and Alex couldn't wait to get to work.

After stopping at the solicitors for Alex to sign the contract subject to finance, they moved to the bank to complete the loan application, then continued to the homestead. There they deposited Sophie and Alex's gear and drove into town.

They had no sooner walked into the bar and exchanged introductions with Ned when he waved a piece of paper at Briony.

'Lola sorted it out for me,' he said as he tapped the side of his nose with an index finger. 'She knew who to talk to and ...' he paused as though about to make a life-changing announcement, 'I can move in at the end of the month!'

Briony squeezed Alex's fingers. She saw the unexpectedly quick acceptance of Ned's application for the council cottage as another sign that purchasing the hotel was the right decision for them all.

Edgy with relief, excitement, and a tiny nagging panic she and Alex may have taken on too much, Briony pushed her worries to the back of her mind and focused on the future. It was already May. In no time, Ned would have moved out and the renovations could begin, provided their finance was approved by then. She acknowledged that they might have to postpone meals for a few days while they thoroughly cleaned and sorted out the kitchen before installing new appliances and benchtops. But, aside from that minor issue, within a month, she and Alex would be the operators of the pub and it would be their names as the licenced publicans on the sign outside. The next job would be to help Ned remove his belongings and go through more than eighty years of accumulated books, photographs, and personal treasures. It was the one job she was dreading.

EVEN WITH THE help of Lola and Frank, Ginny, Kirk, and Ann, sorting and packing a lifetime of Ned's accumulated belongings took days of sifting through long-forgotten items. With limited space in his newly acquired cottage, old clothing, linen, and items that had long since seen better days were removed to Ginny's shed until someone could take them to the recycle centre in Warwick. While Ned packed his favourite books, cooking utensils, and clothing into boxes, he left decades of handwritten hotel diaries for Briony and Alex to trawl through in due course. The pages of these diaries were filled with scrawled booking details in a variety of pencil, faded ink, and modern ballpoint pen.

Finally, Lola oversaw the cleaning of the tiny cottage and assisted Ned in moving in with his belongings.

On the first Saturday after Ned's move, while Alex and Briony operated the bar, most of the town's residents arrived at the pub bearing assorted platters and casserole dishes of food to share. Dining room tables were pushed together to form one long platform that groaned under the weight of food. Ann fussed in the kitchen, supervising her delegated team of reliable teenagers. In a last burst of nostalgia, Ned had handed her a wad of cash, suggesting she "give a few of the local kids a boost if they come and wash the dishes". Lola and Frank's granddaughter, Zoe, had willingly roped in a group of friends, who snapped up the rare opportunity to earn extra money in their own town.

On the evening of his farewell, Lola and Frank flanked Ned in the centre of the hotel dining room. Resplendent in a brand-new shirt and trousers, polished shoes, and with a neatly trimmed beard, the retiring hotelier invited raised eyebrows and congratulations. Even Kirk's eyes widened at the old man's shiny bald skull and beaming smile—a sight rarely seen—as he hovered close in case Ned toppled over under the influence of several "just-a-nip" glasses of whisky.

At last, the remnants of food were cleared away, all shared a chorus of thanks, and a teary Ned sat in the middle of the room as the queue of locals shook his hand and thanked him for the years of hospitality.

It was well after midnight before Alex and Briony fell into bed in the first of the upstairs rooms to have been updated for guests.

A list lay on the bedside table and, as Briony reached over to switch off the light, she picked it up and ran her eye over it. 'Remove floor and wall sheeting in downstairs bedroom—replace, repair, and paint. Is that where we start tomorrow?'

Alex rolled over and shot her a weary look. 'Why not? Only it's not tomorrow because tomorrow is already here.' He held up his wrist so she could read his watch. 'We've got weeks of jobs ahead of us ... and I know the perfect way to begin.'

He reached out and drew her close. Dropping the list on the floor, she gave a soft giggle, snuggled under the doona, and pressed butterfly kisses on his warm skin.

13

———

Sheltered by a tiny synthetic awning, the mesh door glowed with early morning light. Sam crept to the opening and peered out. Surrounding trees dripped moisture onto the saturated ground, but overhead, clear skies shone golden with the rising sun. Incessant rain had continued for three days and, despite the spacious and well-equipped camp kitchen, he'd had enough of being cooped up. He needed space. Freedom. Work.

That's it. I'm bored.

In mute admission that surprised him, he felt a desire for the sun on his back and have his hands and mind busy. It had been weeks since finishing the grape harvest and not only was his patience evaporating, so was his money.

He roused Ciara with a shake of her shoulder.

With a reluctant groan, she muttered, 'What?'

'It's stopped raining. Time to move on.'

She pushed herself to sitting, sweeping dark locks of hair from her face. 'What's the matter with staying here? We haven't explored the entire area yet.'

'Yeah, well, I'm ready to find a job again. Had enough of sitting around.' The words came out more sharply than he meant, but he would not apologise. While his attraction to Ciara remained, her reluctance to contribute to travel costs was worrying him. The whole idea of his taking a year off to travel was to do exactly that. The plan had been to stop when he needed to earn money for the next part of the trip, but to avoid having to dip into his hard-earned savings.

As though reading his mind, Ciara narrowed her eyes. 'Are you running out of money?'

He shrugged. 'It's getting low, but it's not only that. I want to experience other forms of employment while I'm looking around the country. Who knows what it might lead to, and we'll never know what type of career we enjoy most if we don't give a few a try.'

'Suit yourself. I'm telling you now—picking grapes commercially is not something I'll be repeating.' She gathered fresh clothes from her backpack and snatched the damp towel and toiletry bag from the corner of the tent. 'I'm going for a shower.'

Her rigid back, marching across the lawn to the amenity block, confirmed Sam's suspicions. No matter how much he loved her, or thought he did, she wanted control—and until now, he had allowed it.

'No more,' he muttered. 'I need work and I reckon you do too—before you start treating me as a cash cow.' *If I'm not already.*

With renewed vigour and determination, he released the air bed plug and began packing. After stacking everything neatly in the back of the ute, he dashed through the shower and was halfway through cooking the last of the bacon and eggs before Ciara returned.

Mellow and with wide, sparkling eyes, she joined him with an apologetic smile. 'Sorry. You know I'm not the best first thing in the morning. But I'm happy to move on if that's what you want.' Wrapping her arm around his waist, she kissed his cheek.

He slid the contents of the pan onto two plates. 'Righto. After we've eaten, we'll strike the tent and head up to Queensland. Okay?'

'Yep. Provided we stick to the back roads.' Then she plunged a fork into the bacon and filled her mouth.

Sam lifted his face and rolled his eyes at the blue sky. *Whatever.*

CIARA'S INSISTENCE they avoid busy highways turned out to be an excellent decision, and Sam thoroughly enjoyed the journey, slowing to appreciate the glorious late-autumn colours of the trees and freshly washed grass, reminding him of New Zealand. After reaching Stanthorpe, they sat beside Quart Pot Creek and ate lunch before moving on.

Twisting their way over narrow roads clinging to the side of hills, they navigated past ancient timber hay sheds and paddocks of docile-looking cows chewing their cud. Swathes of native bush dotted the landscape, and the air rang with the chime of bellbirds and the chatter of lorikeets.

Bright green crops danced in the breeze as, on the dot of three o'clock, they passed a sign welcoming them to Featherwood Falls before descending onto a bridge. Bubbling water rushed beneath them as they crossed, ending the farmland and morphing into a pretty village. Rows of houses were strung along the hillside and a school and assortment of community facilities nestled against the road.

'Hey, there's a pub.' Sam pointed to the hotel where a young man was pressure-cleaning the front wall of the building. 'Shall we stop and ask if they're looking for workers?'

Ciara shrugged as she glanced around. 'Okay. Looks too quiet to need staff, but you never know.'

Sam pulled to the kerb and parked behind a battered Toyota before opening his door.

When Ciara didn't move, he frowned. 'Coming?'

Slowly sliding out of her seat, Ciara slanted her head and, with narrowed eyes as though she was surveying a crime scene, performed a full three-hundred-and-sixty-degree turn. 'Yes. I think this town will suit us fine for a while.'

Then she smiled at Sam and once again, his heart surged with hope.

The man with the pressure cleaner switched off the machine and dropped the wand on the ground. 'Hello there. Welcome to Featherwood Falls.'

'Gidday,' Sam said. 'You the publican?'

Glancing down at his filthy jeans, the man grinned. 'Yeah, sort of.' He held out his hand. 'Alex Cunningham. My fiancée and I are the managers, soon-to-be owners.'

Returning the handshake, Sam inclined his head toward Ciara. 'This is Ciara—and I'm Sam. We're looking for work ... and somewhere to stay. Do you know if there's anything going around here?'

Alex and Sam studied each other for a moment. 'Could be. Come inside and we'll talk to Briony.'

BRIONY TOOK Sam and Ciara for a tour of the hotel while Alex hovered in the bar, waiting for the late-afternoon patrons to arrive. Briony's insides churned with anticipation. They had barely had a week to adjust to their new life. Now their first employees—except Ann, of course—had turned up out of the blue. It had to be a good omen, especially as both appeared to be experienced and keen to remain in a small, rural environment.

'As you can see, the staff accommodation is not much. But I guess that's why I feel your arrival means it's our lucky day,' Briony said. 'We have a friend starting work on the back rooms tomorrow. Hopefully, they won't take long and then, if you're able to stay on, you could move in to one. For now though ...' She grimaced and pointed to the ceiling. 'There are a couple of rooms upstairs that are comfortable but need painting and new furnishings before we can welcome guests.'

'I'm sure any room will be fine,' Sam replied. 'At least it will be warm and dry.'

Briony beamed at Ciara, delighted to have such an attractive and seemingly enthusiastic worker willing to join them. 'It's perfect you have your RSA certificate. Both Alex and I hoped that, while we get the hotel shipshape at least, we would find someone to take care of the bar for us.'

'I'd love to be that person.' Ciara asked brightly, 'Have you been in hospitality long?'

'A few years. My forte is in management and marketing. Alex is a chef—but we're doing everything at the moment, including tending the bar.' Briony laughed. 'Owning a pub without a bartender wouldn't work well.'

They continued the tour, and the couple selected the best of the upstairs rooms Briony showed them.

'It's unfortunate we can't put you on the payroll immediately. However, it's only a couple more weeks before settlement takes place, which will give us all a chance to get to know one another and ensure you're happy staying here. In the meantime, your food and accommodation will be instead of a wage—and of course will then become part of your employment package if you decide to stay. Does that suit?'

'Sounds good,' Sam said. 'We understand and will be grateful for a solid roof over our heads.'

Ciara tittered. 'We're over camping in pouring rain.'

'I can imagine.' Briony looked at Sam. 'Kirk will be delighted to have another builder onsite to give him a hand, and I'm sure that with your perfectly timed arrival here, we'll have this beautiful old building looking gracious again in no time.'

Briony met Sam's wide beam.

'I'm a cabinet-maker, not a builder—but either way, I'm certain we will.'

14

—————

Sophie talked to the animals as she moved from horse to horse, grooming, cleaning out hooves, and detangling manes and tails.

In the short time since stepping onto Australian shores, she had found her niche—stablehand, cattle musterer, and sheep wrangler. While working along-side Ginny and Kirk on Featherwood Station, she wrestled with wire-strainers to fix damaged fences, trimmed horses' hooves under supervision, and drove the ride-on mower. Of all the skills she had gained in her life, her favourite was working with horses.

As young children, the Cunningham family's quiet pony had tolerated Alex and Sophie's fussing, while Hamish's lack of interest had suited them all. Following Briony's first visit to the small farm, two borrowed Connemara ponies had been installed in their grandpa's front paddock—on loan from an equally aging crofter on the point of Sleat. Sophie, Alex, and Briony had ridden at every opportunity.

Rusty switched his tail, stamping a hoof as she caught the comb in a knot.

'Sorry, old fellow. I'll be more gentle. Not long now and Claire's riding-school business will be in full swing again. Will you enjoy that?' She grinned as the pony blinked his long, black lashes.

While school was in progress, lessons had eased, allowing Claire time to catch up with her graphic design projects. But now with the winter holiday break approaching, Sophie had willingly taken on the duty of maintaining, exercising, feeding, and preparing the equine residents in readiness for the busy period.

'Hey, Sophie!' The call came from somewhere near the kennels.

Lifting her head to the sound, she waved as Ginny approached.

'What's up?'

'I wondered if you'd mind coming to the pub with me this afternoon. I've volunteered us both to help Briony paint the outside walls of the hotel while the weather is good. Kirk and Sam are tackling those back rooms that have to be re-sheeted and floored, and Ciara is taking care of the bar while Alex works on a few new dishes for the restaurant.'

'Sure.' Sophie grinned. 'So, I'm guessing dinner's on Alex tonight?'

Ginny laughed. 'Maybe. I'm sure there will be enough, but if unexpected patrons turn up we can come home and have last night's curry leftovers.'

Sophie looked at her watch. 'I'll finish these horses and let them go, then I'll be in for lunch. I guess we'll need to get down there as early as possible or the paint won't dry before the sun sets?'

'Yes. Do you want a hand?'

'No. I'm fine, thanks.'

'Okay, you're a treasure. I'll make us a sandwich and see you in a few minutes.' Ginny blew her a kiss as she walked away, leaving Sophie filled with a warm glow. Despite Alex's assurance that she would be welcomed in Featherwood Falls, she hadn't expected to feel so at home as she did. Sucking up the courage to relinquish her job in Inverness and come here was possibly one of the best things she'd ever done. As she made her way toward the homestead, Sophie grinned. Despite the excitement of Alex and Briony's new purchase, Sophie had only received a quick tour of the hotel before Alex had served them dinner consisting of his four new menu items. She was yet to meet their new staff, and the thought of being introduced to more travellers filled her with joyful anticipation.

Sophie followed Ginny through the dark timber door into the hotel's interior, glancing at the rear of an orange-shirted customer leaning on the bar, and the bartender facing him. She halted, her jaw slack.

Is that …? It can't be. Alex said her name was Ciara.

The cheery Irish girl was chatting animatedly to the man, and as they drew closer, Ginny gave the girl a wave and continued through the adjoining door to the dining room. Sophie threw a friendly smile toward Ciara, faltering as she received a wary frown in return. Dragging her eyes away, she glanced at Ginny's retreating back before taking another look at the Irish woman.

You look like her, except her hair was a different colour —and longer.

Sophie dredged her mind, recollecting the party she and an old school friend had attended in Inverness months earlier. The slim, straight back reflected in the mirrored row of glass-fronted timber cupboards stirred recollections of a confident woman who had domi-nated the party and successfully ensured Sophie went home that night feeling like an outsider.

'Looking for a drink?' Ciara asked.

Pink heat crept up Sophie's neck. 'No thanks. I'm here to help Briony and Ginny paint. It's just …' She paused for a heartbeat. 'Sorry for staring. You remind me of someone I once met.'

Ciara nodded and returned to continue her conversation with the patron.

At her dismissal, Sophie hurried through the swing door in the direction Ginny had taken, her frown deepening.

'You okay, Sophie?' Briony and Ginny stood beside the kitchen while Briony dried her hands on a tea towel. 'You look worried. I promise we won't work you too hard,' Briony added with a chuckle.

Sophie straightened. 'I'm fine. I thought I recognised your new bartender, but it turns out I was wrong. Amazing how often we have a double somewhere that we don't know about.'

'Too true, although I pity whoever is my double.' Ginny grinned.

'Rubbish, Mum. You're gorgeous—especially for someone over fifty.'

Swinging a hand in a mock slap toward Briony, Ginny said, 'Enough of that. Now. Where do we start?'

As Sophie followed Ginny along the passageway and out into the backyard, her mind tugged her back to the party in Inverness. The music had been loud, and it had been hard to hear anything. Then she shook her head as nervous relief flooded through her.

Of course. Ciara is Irish, and the girl at the party was Australian. I got it wrong.

15

Sophie's attention was drawn to the two men sorting sheets of wall panelling and floorboards on a patch of recently mown grass. One was Kirk, who she had struck an immediate kinship with, while the other—a tanned, well-muscled man with a mop of black, curly hair—must be the other half of the "couple" employed days earlier. Ciara's boyfriend.

Sophie blinked rapidly as he said something to Kirk she couldn't hear. Kirk was a big man, but even he had to look up at his mate. Following the stranger's gaze, Kirk waved and beckoned his assistant to join him as he approached the women.

'Gidday, Ginny, Sophie.' Kirk grinned, his teeth a straight, bright row against the grey-streaked beard.

'Hi, darling. Sam,' Ginny said. Turning to Sophie,

she reached out an arm. 'Sam. This is Sophie, Alex's sister.'

He leaned forward and held out his hand with a friendly smile. She grasped the dry, work-hardened paw, her head tilted back as her eyes met his. Amidst the dark chocolate pools was a spark reflecting her own. For a split second, a jolt of something like electricity ran through her—a strange feeling of intimacy. It was as though they were the only people in the world. A handsome, rugged man and a scrawny, grey-eyed Scotswoman together in the garden of Eden. She opened her mouth to speak, but no words would come.

'Hey, Sophie. Great to meet you.' At the deep, musical tone of Sam's voice, Sophie took a breath, willing her head to stop spinning.

'You too,' she rasped, clearing her throat.

'How are you finding Australia?'

'G-good thanks,' she stuttered. 'You?' *Duh. What a stupid thing to say.*

'Great. It's a good deal bigger and hotter than where I come from, though.'

Sophie stared at him. 'Are you from Tasmania?'

'Nuh. I'm a kiwi. From New Zealand. The land of the long white cloud.' He laughed, and Sophie ducked her head, raising a hand to her throat to quell the rising pink on her pale, northern-hemisphere skin.

She followed his gaze as it swung from the main

street toward the long, gently sloping yard behind the hotel where a stream bubbled over rocks.

Then their eyes met again.

'We haven't been here long, but ...' He grinned again, his face lighting up like the warm glow of a freshly stoked fire. 'Featherwood Falls feels like a pretty good place to stop for a while.'

She nodded mutely, oblivious of her companions.

'You girls ready to start painting?' Kirk asked, snapping Sophie from her dream-bubble. 'Sam and I better get into that damaged room and work out what needs to be done tomorrow.'

Ginny nodded and quipped, 'Do we look the part?' She glanced down at her stained jeans and ragged shirt before inclining her head toward Sophie and Briony. Both girls wore old clothes, Sophie having slipped into a pair of Claire's leggings with the bottoms rolled up and a slightly paint-splattered shirt Ginny had found in the rag bag. 'We wouldn't win "Fashion-on-the-Fields" looking like this ... So, I guess we'd better get started.'

After a flurry of paint-stirring and brush-checking, the three women trekked around the side of the hotel to where Kirk and Sam had set up ladders and trestles.

'I'll start at the top because I'm not afraid of heights,' Briony announced. 'How are you at doing window trims, Sophie?'

Sophie grimaced. 'To be honest, I've never painted

anything except our garden shed at home,' she admitted. 'Dad and my brothers were the painters; Mum and I did the running and fetching and, of course, provided the food.'

'Don't worry,' Ginny said. 'While Briony does the top parts, I'll do the windows and door trims, and you can start halfway down the walls and work toward the ground. Alex has cleaned and prepped the boards, so the paint should flow easily. If we can get the front done this afternoon, tomorrow we'll work on the sides and, within four or five days, I reckon we'll have the place looking beautiful.'

WHILE HER PUZZLED thoughts drifted to Sam and Ciara, Sophie quickly adapted to the new experience—dipping her brush into the paint, wiping just enough off to avoid too many drips on the drop sheets below, and swiping the brush evenly along the horizontal weatherboards.

After what felt like hours later, she paused, dropped her brush into the empty paint container, and rubbed her shoulders as the afternoon sun began to fade. Stepping back, she analysed their afternoon's work.

'What do you think?' Ginny asked as she came to stand beside her.

'It looks fabulous. Amazing how a coat of paint can make a building look like new again.'

'I know. Once we get the outside done, we'll freshen up these sad-looking tubs and plant flowers.'

Sophie glanced at the four large half-barrels parked haphazardly, like forgotten shopping trolleys at the end of the building. Semi-filled with dirt, they held only weeds and dozens of cigarette butts. She silently agreed they did nothing to enhance the appeal of the hotel.

Briony climbed down from the trestles, stretching her back as she studied their work. 'Impressive what three women can achieve in an afternoon, especially as half the town seems to have passed by and felt the need to stop and comment.'

With an amused laugh, she beckoned Sophie and her mother to follow her and led them across the road where they stood admiring the building, astounded at the improvement a simple application of fresh, cream-coloured paint had made. Although the hotel had had a vaguely cream appearance, its previous coat of paint had been decades ago, and any remaining colour had become stained with dirt and age, resulting in a faded and shabby look.

'I reckon that's enough for today.' Ginny hooked her arm through Sophie's elbow. 'We need to get home to feed the animals and give the dogs a run before it's too dark.'

They strolled back to the hotel and gathered up the remnants of paint, brushes, and drop sheets before following the narrow, cobbled pathway around the side of the building into the rear yard.

Tired and relieved to be returning to the farm—away from the disconcerting emotions that bubbled inside her—Sophie washed her brush under the rusted tap precariously attached to a corrugated-iron water tank. When all the painting equipment was clean, she followed Briony and Ginny toward the back veranda.

She had barely stepped a foot on the timber boards when an expletive that her mother would have scowled at emanated from the room under repair at the opposite end of the veranda.

'Are you okay?' Kirk boomed, drawing all three women toward the door of the back room.

They huddled against the frame and Sophie peered over Briony's shoulder. Her breath caught in a gasp. Amidst a cloud of dust, Sam's upper body was visible, while his legs seemed to have vanished beneath the floor.

Sam hauled himself out and rested awkwardly on the rough edges of the hole, his eyes bulging. For several seconds, his dazed stare roved around his audience before he leaned forward and peered into the ground below. 'I-I.' He shook his head. 'I landed on something that cracked—like wood. Must be another layer of boards under this one—like a cellar, perhaps?' He looked at Briony questioningly.

'I don't think there's a cellar in this place?' Briony's forehead creased. "Ned never mentioned it anyway—and he lived here his whole life.'

'One way to find out,' Kirk said. He pulled a face mask from his pocket and settled it into place before waving Sam aside and lying on his belly. Reaching into the hole, he then removed several pieces of broken timber and passed them to Sam, who laid them carefully on the floor behind him.

Minutes ticked by as they waited for the dust to settle, then, after stabilising the floor with long planks that had been stacked in the room's corner, Kirk kneeled beside the hole again, the torch on his phone lighting up the cavity. With hair shrouded in dust and his dark eyes widening with disbelief, he turned and beckoned Sam. 'Look.'

As the women remained poised, waiting in mute silence for an explanation, a noisy gasp rose from Sam.

'What is it?' Briony pushed between them, glanced down, and then looked back at Ginny and Sophie, her face masked in horror.

Both Ginny and Sophie moved forward cautiously and dropped to their knees. Bending forward, Sophie took a moment to register the objects lying in the dust below. As recognition registered, her eyes locked with Ginny's in shock.

'Is it—?' Ginny paused for a beat. 'Is it what I think it is?'

Kirk nodded slowly. 'Yep. A termite-eaten box holding a skeleton. And if I'm right, it's not an animal. It's the bones of a baby.'

16

Her exhaustion forgotten, Sophie followed the others to the empty dining room agreeing they needed a seat most while they worked out what to do, especially since they were now covered in a fine, powdery dust.

While Sam and Kirk moved additional chairs around the biggest table, Alex checked Ciara was coping with the bar before joining the group. They sat down and began.

'The first thing we need to do is involve Rhys,' Kirk said firmly. 'As the local cop, he will know about procedures for this sort of thing.'

'I imagine forensics will have to be involved, and perhaps James and his detective team,' Ginny added.

Minutes later, Briony, Alex, and Kirk headed for the police station, Sam returned to the back room to ensure the floor was clear and as safe as possible for the expected deluge of interested parties, and Ginny and Sophie were on their way back to Featherwood Station.

'Who do you think the baby might belong to ... that is, if it's confirmed to be a human baby?' Sophie allowed doubt to creep into her voice. It all seemed too devastating to be true. Perhaps not so rare in archaeological sites in Scotland, but here? Under the floorboards of a small country hotel? She shuddered.

'I really don't know,' Ginny answered thoughtfully. 'Lola might know more, but I think Ned's parents bought the pub sometime between World War One and World War Two. I suspect that'll be one of the first things asked by whoever takes the case. They'll probably question every family who had a relative living here in the past.

'That is—unless they believe the death is more recent.'

Ginny shot a wide-eyed glance at Sophie. 'I don't think so. Did you notice the scraps of material around the bones? Only tiny bits, but they had that open-weave texture of hessian sacking ... like the ones they used for vegetables and anything farm-related before plastic was invented.

Sophie sucked in a noisy breath. 'Listen to us. Anyone would think we're part of Agatha Christie's books.'

'You're right—and I'm Miss Marple.'

Their lighthearted moment lasted only seconds before each receded into solemn silence, the car creeping slowly along the driveway.

BY NINE O'CLOCK THE following morning, vehicles filled the hotel car park while the veranda and dining room swarmed with white and blue-shrouded officials, their faces and extremities encased in masks, gloves, and booties.

Ciara bounced around the bar area, wiping tables and plying everyone who entered with warm hospitality, as though each was the most important in the world.

After much discussion, photography, and delicate, precise handling, the fragments of a handmade oak box and the pathetic remains of the little human were carefully laid in containers, labelled, and carried to a waiting vehicle.

Sam stood beside Briony, his eyes and ears tuned to every comment, straining to overhear the conversation between the detective team and the forensic officer. Sadness filled his chest and drove a dull ache deep into his belly. What had happened all that time ago to make a young mother—or someone else— bury their precious baby under a building? Why hadn't the child been laid to rest in the local cemetery instead?

'I'll get the report back to you as soon as possible.' An older gentleman, who Sam had heard introduced to Alex as Forensic Officer Robert Malcolm, stood between Alex and another man.

'That's Detective Senior Constable James Avery beside Alex,' Briony murmured. 'He's lovely—and efficient.' She paused for a few moments. 'He was the guy who helped us solve the cause of my dad's death—and he's led the team that cleaned the drug cartel out of our valley.'

Sam stared at her, reeling at the sorrow that edged her tone. Since arriving in Featherwood Falls, his respect and admiration for Briony and Alex had grown. At first, he had assumed they were a young couple who wanted to give a new idea a go—to restore and then flip a run-down hotel they'd picked up cheaply before moving on to bigger and better things. But now he understood how the tight-knit community and the beauty of the valley wormed its way inside visitors—and Briony was no visitor. She had grown up here and was deeply invested in the town's past, present, and future.

It was late afternoon before the site was cleared for Sam and Kirk to continue working in the room, and by then, Kirk declared his deteriorating eyesight made further work too difficult. 'It'll be dark soon—best to get a fresh start in the morning.' He squinted, and Sam followed his gaze down the backyard. 'How about you and I make the most of the remaining daylight and clear a path to the creek? This yard is a mess.'

Sam nodded, pleased to hear the untidiness was getting someone else down as well as him. The vegetation was patchy: long in places entwined with weeds and rubbish, with the balance being bare dirt with clumps of khaki burr threatening to take over.

A session operating a brush-cutter and lawn mower with earmuffs on was just what he needed. Perhaps then he could sort out why his stupid mind kept seeing a slight, grey-eyed young woman instead of Ciara, the girl he had been certain he loved only a few weeks earlier. He had never been in love before. He had never even had a long-time girlfriend. Now a ripple of doubt filtered through him. Was what he felt for Ciara nothing more than lust? The bright, effervescent personality she'd shown him initially had cracked, and he had witnessed another side of her—a moody, impoverished Irishwoman depending on him. Had it all been a façade?

His stomach roiled with embarrassment and dread. Perhaps he was nothing more than a lovesick idiot a long way from home.

17

______

'I've got our first guest booking!' Briony shouted over the noise of the food processor.

Switching off the appliance, Alex looked up, a grin spreading across his open, freckled face. 'Told you as soon as we got this place shipshape, the word would get around. Is it someone important—like a television crew wanting to put us on the map?'

Briony rolled her eyes. 'If it was, I would be in a much bigger panic than I am already.'

'Why are you worrying? You've done a great job in the bedrooms. And the bathrooms are finished except for some touch-up painting.'

'Yeah. I know. I just want everything to be perfect and they're not. I'm pleased Kirk changed that poky little single room into a dual-entry ensuite though.

Gives us the option for someone exactly like this guest to have more privacy.' She looked down at her notes. 'She's a woman travelling on her own—mature from the sound of her voice. Apparently, she knows Zoe, Lola, and Frank's granddaughter. Used to live next door or something.'

'Is she coming to visit Zoe?'

'I guess so. She said something about researching her family history in the region. I suppose she thought it would be a chance to visit Zoe and check out the area while she was here? Anyway, she's booked in for an entire week, so I'll give her the room with the floral doona cover and curtains, and she can have solo use of the ensuite.'

'Sounds good.' Alex appeared to have lost interest as he emptied the contents of the food processor into a bowl and focused on measuring ingredients.

Accepting her dismissal, Briony returned to the tiny office between the bar and kitchen. It was the one room that had required little attention, as it appeared it had been rarely used. Rows of leather-bound annual diaries filled the top shelves dating from 1930 onwards, while closer to the built-in timber desk, more modern-looking books lined up in perfect precision from the nineteen nineties through to the twenty-twenties. The current yearbook lay open next to Briony's laptop.

Eleanor Worth, she wrote before ruling a line across from next Monday to the following Sunday. Despite having set up an appropriate software package on her laptop to record bookings, something made her follow the historical example and enter the information into the diary in her neatest handwriting. *This is an important booking—our very first*, she reasoned. *Thank goodness the police have given permission for the floor to be finished downstairs.* After the initial flurry of questions and interest, they had heard no more from the police except that they would let her know if they needed to return.

Briony hoped that by the time Mrs Worth arrived, Sam and Ciara would have moved into the room currently under renovation. By then, the tiny bathrooms that served dining and bar customers and staff would have also been repainted. The new stainless-steel benches and large gas cooktop ordered for the kitchen would take a little longer.

Briony pressed her thumbs and fingertips together, forming a diamond shape, and quietly sighed. The newly painted exterior with its tubs of flowers decorating the entrance was welcoming, while the inside had received a thorough clean and the rustic floorboards had been sanded and re-coated. Vases of perfumed flowers from Ginny's garden adorned the dining tables, giving the room a fresh, inviting air. *I'm being silly.* The hotel really looked lovely—even so, she twitched with impatience.

She ran her finger down the list in her diary as a

familiar "Yoo-hoo" sounded from the hotel entrance. It was at least half an hour before opening time, but it had become habit to unlock the doors when they came down for breakfast, even if that was six o'clock. Both Briony and Alex reasoned it was not only their hotel, but it was also their home and if visitors wanted to pop in to see them, the last thing they would want was for a locked door to turn them away.

A grin spread across her face as she dashed into the hallway and was encompassed in Lola's generous hug.

'Hello, love.' Lola took a step back, holding Briony's upper arms and tut-tutting. 'You look tired.'

Briony grunted. 'Yeah, well ... it's been a busy six weeks.'

'Let's have a cuppa and a chat. I came to tell you that the lady who lived across the hall from Zoe in Brisbane is coming to Featherwood Falls.' Lola beamed.

'I know. She's phoned and made a booking to stay here.'

Lola's face seemed to deflate. 'Of course. I didn't realise she would ring so soon. She only sent a message to Zoe at breakfast time this morning.' Distractedly, she swung her gaze around the room. 'Your helpers not here?'

'No. It's their day off today. Poor things. They've worked solidly since they arrived and wanted to have a couple of days to hike in Girraween.' She shrugged, then grinned at Lola. 'Can you believe it? We've been in this beautiful place for a month now and even have paid staff.'

Lola chuckled as they entered the kitchen and slumped into chairs that surrounded the rectangular table in the corner of the room. 'Real life for you and Alex is only just beginning.'

WITH A MUG of tea in front of them, Briony fixed her gaze on the woman who had been a pseudo grand-mother, a friend, and an advisor for as long as Briony could remember. It had been Lola she and Claire went to for advice if they felt Ginny was too busy, preoccu-pied, or their problem involved an issue they didn't want to tell their mother about. Lola had also been their biggest supporter at every sporting event they entered, every school concert and presentation evening, and had been the shoulder all the Shepherd women had cried on following Lyndon's death. Briony's love for Lola was deep and respectful.

'I've been thinking about your opening.'

Briony blinked, wondering for a second what Lola was talking about. The pub was already open. 'The opening?'

'You know—the "spit roast and invite the whole town" party you mentioned when Ned agreed to sell you the hotel.' Lola held her hands up, her fingers imitating quotation marks.

'Of course,' Briony said. 'We've been so busy getting the place looking nice, I haven't really thought about it again.'

'Well, I have.' Lola beamed, her spine straightening as she lifted her chin. 'I think it's an excellent idea. Of course, we will help—and we'll get Zoe and her friends to spread the word by whichever means you choose. She offered to work with Claire to create a flyer for the shop window and a letterbox drop. You know how quickly news travels in small towns.'

'Hang on a tick.' Briony laid her hand on Lola's arm. 'I think you're getting ahead of yourself.'

A tiny frown crept over Lola's forehead. 'In what way?'

'Well, the renovations aren't finished yet. We still don't have the kitchen up to industry standard—although that should be done in the next two weeks—and what about the body?'

'The body?' Lola's eyes widened for a moment before she huffed out a breath, relaxing into her seat again. 'You mean the baby.'

'Yes, of course. The police are still investigating it and the coroner's report is ages away yet. Rhys told Claire and Claire told me that they'll probably ask for DNA samples from any family member who has been in the area for generations. Plus, we've had journalists ring up and gossip columnists call in.'

Lola narrowed her eyes. 'How do you know they're gossip columnists?'

'Because they amble into the bar in their office clothes, order a drink, and then start chatting to Ciara as though she's a long-lost friend. She's outgoing and possibly naïve, even though we've talked about keeping things quiet. So, she tells them everything she knows—and I suspect they trot away and dash off a juicy piece of prose that includes what we know and a good bit of what we don't.'

'Have you got evidence of this?'

'Not really. Only a snippet that Ashleigh showed me from the free community paper.'

Lola snorted. 'I think you're being too precious. That paper covers an enormous area, and anyway, don't you think it's helping put this place on the map?'

'Maybe. But it seems like it's for the wrong reasons.'

Drawing a deep breath, Lola shook her head. 'It's an unfortunate and tragic discovery, but I don't believe it will affect your trade or the popularity of this hotel negatively. Of course it will bring speculation and interest. We're human after all … But if you change your mindset, I think you and Alex could turn this into a positive. Have a big celebration—a rebirth—of this lovely building and bring in all you can to showcase the history and tranquillity of our town.'

She paused for a moment as their eyes met and they laughed.

'Tranquillity? Yeah, a gorgeous little valley that just happens to have had a run of problems—drug cartels, manslaughter, bushfires, and my uncle imprisoned,' Briony spluttered. 'All we need now is a massive flood and we've just about seen it all.'

'Don't even think about it. I know there've been floods in the past, but now we have good bridges, culverts, and flood mitigation—according to the council, anyway. If we get torrential rain, there will be minimal damage and our homes will be safe.' Lola twisted her mouth ruefully. 'Let's hope they're right.'

Briony inclined her head toward the window where the early winter sun streamed through the glass, resting its golden glow on the newly polished floor. 'No chance of rain today.'

'No,' Lola said firmly. 'So, what's it going to be? Shall we say around the middle of July, you'll host a community spit-roast dinner here at the pub to celebrate new beginnings?'

A leap of excited anticipation filled Briony. Perhaps this was just what Featherwood Falls required—and what she and Alex needed to do in order to display their professionalism, good food, and share their friendly atmosphere. Sam and Ciara were perfect employees, and she was sure that with the support of her family and friends, a mid-winter warm-up would kick their business off perfectly.

She gave Lola a huge grin. 'You're on.'

FOR THE REST of the day, Briony's head buzzed with excitement as she made numerous calls to Lola and Claire with suggestions and approvals. The thought of creating an event for her own business was invigorating despite the challenges.

While Alex prepared vegetables and delicious-smelling sauces for both the range of takeaway meals he had introduced and the evening menu, Briony ran through her list, accepting his brief nods as approval.

'We'll have the fires burning in the bar and dining rooms for ambience and warmth—and Lola said she'd ask Valerie and Neil at Kallala if we can borrow their outdoor gas heaters and a stack of the chairs they use for weddings. I'll talk to Kirk and Sam and see if they could build a fire pit out the back with plenty of seating around it. Mum said she and Sophie have potted up a heap of winter-flowering plants that can fill in bare corners around the veranda—and ...' She paused for a minute, waiting for Alex to meet her gaze.

When he did, he raised an eyebrow. 'And?'

'What do you think about us putting in a fantastic wood-fired pizza oven out the back as well?'

For a few moments, Alex's face remained emotionless, his blue eyes glazed as though allowing his thoughts to ruminate. Then he grinned, his freckled face alight. 'Sounds like a great idea. What are Kirk's skills like at producing one?'

'Not sure, but I'll soon find out.'

She threw an arm around Alex's neck and kissed him on the cheek before dashing from the kitchen, her thick brown hair swinging around her shoulders.

18

———

Sam sagged onto the air bed, charged with high spirits although spent of energy.

'I'm knackered.' Ciara threw herself down beside him before rolling onto her back and staring at the tent roof.

'Maybe that hike to the top of The Pyramid last night was a bit much. I loved it though, and you did say you wanted to watch the sunset—and sunrise this morning.'

'No comment.'

Sam laughed. They had left Featherwood Falls early the previous day, and by nine in the morning they'd had their tent pitched and were setting off on their first trail. Having had almost three weeks in the hotel, spending time off sleeping or catching up with movies on Sam's laptop, Ciara had lost some of her fitness. By lunchtime, she had been lagging farther and farther behind, so they had agreed to return to camp for a rest then pack a salad and cold meat and hike to the top of The Pyramid to watch the sunset. Returning after dark had been easier than Sam expected, with Ciara seemingly too preoccupied with following his footsteps to grumble about sore muscles. Then, as they'd sat under the tent awning sipping tea and staring at the myriad of stars lighting up the Milky Way, she had announced they should return to the top in the morning to watch the sunrise.

Sam had been both delighted and surprised. Although their days in the hotel were long, they weren't particularly hard. Being outdoors surrounded by the fresh scent of native bush and breathtaking views was more than a man needed to revive ... only he hadn't been entirely sure Ciara agreed.

With winter rolling in, the days were shorter, so it had been almost six in the morning before they bundled out of the tent again and began their trek to the massive balancing rock near the summit of The Pyramid.

Sam clasped his hands behind his head and let his mind return to the morning's events. The crisp air had been whisper-quiet, the early frost blanketing the ground around the campsite as they set off in total darkness. It had seemed too magical to break the spell, so they had sat for over an hour, drinking in the colours transforming from pale gold to deep apricot before fingers of red brightened the dark blue sky and the sun's rays touched the horizon. Ciara had spoken first, complaining of a numb backside, so Sam had hauled her to her feet and they had continued to explore another two of the shorter walks in the park.

'Let's stop in Stanthorpe for lunch,' Ciara interrupted his reminiscences.

He rolled onto his side, their eyes meeting. A flash of uncertainty surfed through him as he studied her determined, almost challenging expression. He nodded in silent agreement and pushed himself up to a sitting position.

The time had come for them to pack up and start their journey back to Featherwood Falls—and although he had enjoyed the two-day break, he was taken aback by how much he was looking forward to returning.

DESPITE THEIR RELATIVELY COMPANIONABLE days together, Sam relished being back at work and was keen to complete the wall lining in the two rear rooms of the hotel. While Ciara resumed her place behind the bar—one which seemed to suit both the clientele and Ciara well.

The local authority had approved the conversion of

the ancient washhouse in the yard adjacent to the back veranda to unisex bathrooms, each with a shower, toilet, and vanity unit. Sam was looking forward to completing the two rooms so he and Ciara could move downstairs and have accommodation away from any guests who booked in—and the areas Briony and Alex had claimed as their retreat.

A worried frown crept over Sam's forehead as his thoughts drifted to his partner. His uncertainty had grown since their days in Girraween. Was she the right girl for him? Why did she seem evasive whenever he suggested it was her turn to pay for their lunch? He hadn't dared ask why she needed to take her toiletry bag everywhere with her, even when hiking. She rarely stared into his eyes anymore, but when she did there was something deep in hers that he couldn't read. Did she love him as she said she did? Or was she hiding something that could destroy the relationship he had worked hard to maintain?

The drill screeched as he pressed against the last sheet of panel board. He jumped, almost catching his thumb when Ciara tapped on his shoulder.

'Sorry. Didn't mean to give you a fright,' she said.

'What's up?' He glanced at the two mugs of coffee she held in one hand.

'Nothing. Taking my break, that's all. Thought I'd come and sit in the sun for a while.'

'Okay. Give me a minute to get this board on and I'll join you.'

Perched on the edge of the veranda with legs dangling, they faced the neatly trimmed grass that had flourished since the removal of the rank clumps of weeds and woody scrub. Beyond the swathe of grass now burned to the colour of honey by frost, the stream was visible. Rushes and assorted rocks worn smooth from years of being tumbled among their granite companions lined the sides of the creek, while the gentle burble of water rushing by reached his ears.

'It's nice here, isn't it?' Sam breathed before taking a gulp of his coffee.

'It's okay.'

He swivelled his gaze to meet her dark-lashed eyes, their tiny pupils almost swallowed by the sapphire irises. When they had first met, she only had to blink to make him jump. Now they triggered a wariness within him—a feeling of walking on eggshells.

'What do you mean?'

'Yeah. It's nice. But there's plenty of places in the world that are nicer.' Her tone was dismissive.

'I guess there are.'

In silence, he finished his coffee and handed her the mug.

'Sorry, gotta get back to it. I want to paint the room tomorrow ...' He pointed to the old washhouse. 'Then work on that. Briony's got the plumber booked for Friday, so Kirk and I've got to be ready.'

'We'll use the bathroom upstairs if it's not. At least if this room is finished, we can set ourselves up here and have some privacy.'

Sam wasn't so sure about that—and it had nothing to do with privacy for him. The thought of what had occurred in the room many years earlier troubled him. Had the baby been born here? Did it die right where he and Ciara would sleep—that is, if they were still together? And what about the mother?

He tried to shake the thoughts from his mind, reminding himself that Ned's parents had slept in the room for decades, followed by Ned and his wife, presumably blissfully unaware of the history only a metre beneath the floorboards. Briony had reassured him that Ned made no mention of ghosts or ill-feeling.

His eyes roved over the layout of the area while he forced his mind away from the room, instead reminding himself of his desire to spend as long as it took to spruce the place up and help Briony and Alex realise their dream. Once he had achieved that, he would fulfil his own yearning and head north so he could see more of Queensland before his year ran out.

Returning to drilling and hammering, he breathed a relieved sigh that the inside facilities had been a quick and easy job thanks to the large, relatively new septic system outside. While Ned had been reluctant to spend money on his business, there had been some areas where he had been given no choice.

TWO DAYS LATER, both the room where the unsettling discovery had been made and the one opposite where Ned had slept were finished, the walls painted in pristine white with the floorboards stained a glossy nut brown. In each room, a window faced out onto the backyard, while one interior wall now sported a built-in wardrobe complete with shelving, hanging space, and drawers. A ceiling fan and small temperature control unit had been installed for comfort in all conditions, and Briony had ordered two new Queen-sized ensembles for the upstairs rooms while Sam and Alex transferred the older beds downstairs to the staff quarters.

'Do you want to help me shift our gear before you start?' Sam asked Ciara, as she brushed her dark hair and tied it in a high ponytail.

'I can't. I'm needed at the bar in a few minutes. You move it. I've put most of my stuff in my rucksack anyway and can get the rest later.'

He nodded, shrugging. For someone who had seemed desperate to move downstairs "closer to the action" days earlier, she seemed to have lost interest. He had assumed she wanted to be closer to the bar so she could duck into their room and fix her hair or makeup without having to run the conspicuous gauntlet of nipping upstairs.

She gave him a quick kiss and flew out the door, leaving him surrounded with rumpled bedding and a pile of dirty washing. He glanced around. Her rucksack may have been packed, but she had left makeup, shoes, and a dressing gown scattered over the bed and floor.

He moved to the wardrobe and began loading his own items into his backpack. It was dark and cloying inside the cupboard; the powerful smell of Ciara's perfume mixed with a hint of mould and old timber.

Accepting he needed better light if he was to sort things out properly, he dragged everything onto the bedroom floor and began putting items into piles before packing his belongings neatly.

An indistinguishable black plastic bag was the last item to see the daylight. Frowning, Sam upended it, allowing a tangle of clothing to spill onto the floor. A small, blue vinyl bag the size of a large pencil case poked out from beneath a brightly coloured garment —a boho-style dress he had not seen Ciara wear. He extracted the case, his heart pounding with guilt. These were Ciara's belongings and not something he had any right to inspect. Except to fetch a jacket for her if she had requested it, he had never touched her things—despite the chaos they were frequently left in, which usually triggered a frustrated groan from him as he swept them off his side of the bed. But this didn't look like a toiletry or makeup bag, and curiosity got the better of him. Resembling a large wallet, could it be somewhere she kept her passport? Or perhaps it was for her money?

He chuckled to himself at the thought of Ciara having the cash to stash anywhere. Any wallet she owned would be empty. This one was fat. He picked it up and slid the zip open.

The amusing thoughts disappeared in a heartbeat.

Unable to believe what he was seeing, he carefully prised the contents out of the wallet and laid them on the floor in front of him.

Money. A huge wad of cash. He flicked through the pile, confirming it was Australian currency and was a mix of both hundred- and fifty-dollar notes. *There's got to be ten grand here.* He let his breath out between his teeth with a quiet whistle.

Was Ciara lying about her lack of money? Or did this belong to someone else? Someone who had stayed in their room long ago?

After running a hand over the wallet he lifted it to his nose, confirming it still wore the smell of new vinyl. Shaking his head, he dropped it back on the floor: it had to be his or Ciara's. It certainly wasn't his.

Sitting back on his heels, he stared at the proof, puzzled over why she had lied to him. He hadn't questioned her too deeply when she'd professed to be broke with the excuse of having to send money to her family. Provoking a tongue-lashing from her was not something he'd wanted to do.

A passport caught his eye and he reached out to extract it, shocked when his fingers brushed against not one but two familiar booklets—one navy blue and one a deep red.

He opened them, laying them side by side—one Australian and the other Irish with almost identical photos of the passport holder. *I guess that's not unusual. I know people with more than one passport.* Then he registered the details and his jaw dropped. Ciara King and Naomi Kelly. He quickly checked the covers to establish which one belonged to the Ciara he knew. He squinted at each, establishing the photo in Naomi's Australian passport was the woman sharing a room with him, while the photo in the Irish document was very similar—but not identical.

Questions circled in his head while an icy chill filtered through his veins. *Is Ciara who she says she is? And if she is, then who is Naomi Kelly and where is she?*

Footsteps outside jolted him to the present. Recognising Briony's determined march, he held his breath while she continued briskly down the hall before snapping a photo of each passport with his phone. Running a finger along the inside of the wallet to check what else may be inside it, he touched something hard. He grasped it and pulled out a small piece of plastic. A credit card? Flipping it over, the details confirmed it was a debit card in Ciara's name—but one for a bank he didn't recognise. Taped to it was a tiny sim card—one compatible with an early model android phone. An item Ciara had declared she did not own.

When he and Ciara had first met, her reasoning for not having a mobile had been that she didn't like social media and preferred to contact her family through public phones. Although surprised and puzzled by the revelation, he hadn't pursued it as she'd added the almost unheard explanation, *I prefer to be free, and that includes not allowing a device to control me.*

Footfalls hurried past the door again, thrusting his attention away from his discovery. He slid the money back into the wallet along with the passports, card, and sim before dropping it into the black plastic bag. Then he added the assortment of clothing he had pulled out earlier and placed the plastic bag in the corner of the room beside her rucksack. While continuing to pack his own belongings, he struggled to drag his thoughts from the contents of the blue wallet. Would Ciara hide it somewhere when she unpacked her gear in the new bedroom? Or would she casually throw it in the wardrobe as she had done here. He hoped so. He needed time to process his thoughts without suspicion.

19

Sophie looked up from the flower bed at the approaching vehicle, her handful of weeds poised midair. The fading sun shed its golden light over the paddocks, highlighting the changing effects early frosts had made on the grass, turning the blades from green to shades of caramel.

A door slammed and Rhys strode through the little gate, hurried up the path, and took the steps two at a time.

Curious about his urgency, she got to her feet and followed him, stripping off gloves and tucking them into her jacket pocket. Arriving in the living area at the same time as Claire appeared from the hallway, Sophie swung her glance between the two of them. Rhys appeared agitated—serious, with the air of someone who was about to announce something important.

Ginny was stirring a pot on the stove, the fragrance of meat and herbs drifting around the room. The older woman hesitated for a beat before turning the element off and resting her hands on the countertop, her eyes fixed on her son-in-law.

'Thought you'd like to know—James rang. I was coming back from a call out so popped in to tell you rather than ringing,' Rhys announced.

'About the baby?' Claire's voice wore a low, concerned edge. 'Is there news?'

Immediately after discovering the tiny skeleton at the hotel, Sophie's thoughts had been consumed by it. But now her days were filled with caring for the horses and dogs, helping move cattle and sheep to fresh paddocks, and convincing Ginny that she was perfectly capable of operating the ride-on mower and weeding gardens. No matter how much she tried to push the thoughts away, she had also been consumed with others involving a certain tall, wild-haired man with eyes the colour of chocolate.

'Yes. He said he'd pop into the pub tonight to talk to us about their findings. Is that okay?'

'Of course. I'll ring Briony.' Ginny indicated the pot on the stove. 'I've made a goulash for dinner, so we can save that for tomorrow night and have a pub meal instead. Chat while we eat—if that suits James, of course.'

Rhys grinned. 'I'm sure it will. We've got a couple of

other matters to catch up on first, but ... let's say six o'clock in the dining room?'

'Okay by me,' Ginny answered, raising an eyebrow at Claire and Sophie.

Claire shrugged. 'Sure.'

'Right then. I'd better get back to the station and I'll see you at the pub.'

He took a step toward Claire and kissed her before shooting out the door and leaping down the steps like a startled deer.

Sophie glanced from Claire to Ginny, a thread of anticipation mixing with the lump of dread in her stomach. 'I wonder what they've discovered.'

'So do I,' Claire echoed.

For a few seconds, they looked at each other before Ginny swung her gaze to the kitchen clock. 'It's nearly five. Sophie, would you mind leaving the gardening now? Perhaps you could feed the dogs and chooks before it gets dark. I'll finish this goulash and jump through the shower.'

'I need to complete the design I'm doing but shouldn't be long. Then I'll nip home and meet you all at the pub.' Claire peered through the French doors. 'Where's Kirk?'

'He's cleaning the woolshed ready for crutching. I'm sure he would have seen Rhys's car so will be up soon.'

Each spun in a different direction and hurried off

to complete their respective duties with renewed purpose in their strides.

AN HOUR LATER, wearing clean jeans and a bottle-green woollen jumper, courtesy of her mother's passion for knitting, Sophie followed Kirk and Ginny into the hotel dining room.

Rhys and Claire sat opposite an older man Sophie assumed was James, the detective who had attended the discovery. His smile was brief as Rhys introduced her before he shook Kirk's hand and kissed Ginny on the cheek. Sophie relaxed a little, recognising the concerned look and deep lines in the kind, crumpled face as those of a man who took his job seriously.

Briony had been attending the bar when they walked in. But within a few minutes, both Briony and Alex arrived, announcing Ann was looking after the evening meals and Ciara and Sam were taking care of the patrons. Disappointment that Sam wasn't joining the family spiked Sophie's concentration, and she nearly missed James's question.

'Sophie. What would you like to drink?'

'Umm. Lemon, lime, and bitters, please.'

With the drinks requests sorted, James and Rhys left the room to order and Sophie breathed deeply, desperate to regain a calm appearance, despite her insides paddling frantically like a duck on a pond.

After what seemed to her to have been an unnecessarily long time, everyone was finally seated with a beverage in front of them, dinner had been ordered, and James could share his report.

'Forensics have established the child was a newborn baby girl. She may have been stillborn as she was small—possibly premature, and it is possible there was a medical issue as tests revealed a deformed spinal cord.'

'Spina bifida or something similar?' Ginny asked.

He nodded. 'They think so.'

'Could they tell how long ago she was born?' Claire asked.

James rocked back in his chair and cleared his throat. 'Apparently, it's difficult to define the exact time, but they suspect she had been there for over eighty years.'

'Hooley Dooley!' Kirk's eyes widened. 'So that puts her death at somewhere in the thirties, probably close to the outbreak of the Second World War.'

James nodded again. 'Yes, that's what they're thinking. So ... as they can extract DNA, they now start searching for a family or blood tie—if only to provide the child with a surname for a proper burial. Of course, Ned has been informed as it is possible the child is related, given that his parents purchased this hotel around that time.'

'What do you need from us?' Claire asked.

'We'll begin here. We all know how news travels fast in the country, so I know there will be a lot of local people already wondering. If those who know they had family living in or around this area about then agree to come forward, we'll be questioning them and will take DNA samples from those who seem possibilities. Ned is suffering from mild shock but will be the first to assist by providing a DNA sample.'

'That includes us too, doesn't it?' Claire swung her gaze from her sister to her mother. 'I mean, we should line up to give DNA, seeing as our family has been here for even longer than Ned's.'

'Absolutely.' Ginny's eyes narrowed. 'I don't remember your grandfather talking about a connection with the hotel, though. Back then, I think the timber cutters and the few miners that remained in the area used the pub more. It wasn't a place for a family ...' She paused for a moment as a frown deepened. 'But your great-grandfather was a tough man and had a lot of influence in the town. I imagine he would have been a frequent visitor to this place.'

Briony gasped. 'Are you suggesting he could be responsible for that poor little baby? That we could actually be related to it ... her?'

Shrugging, Ginny reached out and lay a hand on Briony's. 'Don't get upset, love. We know your great-grandmother wasn't the only woman in his life. Let's just do our best to help the police with this—and put whatever the findings are down to history, no matter the outcome.'

Briony rolled her eyes at Claire while Sophie's gaze darted from face to face, thankful she wasn't a family member. Something stirred inside her—a question never asked. Did her own family have hidden secrets? It hadn't occurred to her, but now she thought about it, perhaps they did and perhaps one day, those secrets would surface and affect her family as much as this discovery had the potential to do to the Shepherds.

'I'm going to have a look through the storeroom and see if I can find any police records or diaries for the 1930s,' Rhys announced. 'They helped us when we were searching for information on that old miner whose bones were found up on the Camel Hump. You never know. Some bored cop back in those days might have noted something that gives us a clue.'

Ann arrived with their meals and the conversation stalled.

The door between the dining room and bar swung open, and Sam strode into the room. 'Hi all.' His cheery grin flashed around the group before resting on Sophie.

'Hi,' she squeaked.

'Are you joining us for dinner, Sam?' Alex indicated

the spare chair next to Sophie. 'Sit down and I'll let Ann know you're here.'

Sam waved a hand and took a step toward the kitchen. 'I'll nip in and save her the walk. The bar's pretty quiet, so Ciara insisted I grab the opportunity while it's there. She said she's not hungry but will pop in later and get something.'

Secretly delighted that Sam was going to hang around, Sophie blushed when he returned and sat beside her, his plate laden with steaming chicken schnitzel and vegetables.

Her appetite suddenly evaporated, and she played with the rest of her meal, unable to finish the man-sized serving Ann had dished up.

'How's it all going, Sophie? Enjoying yourself?' Sam's voice was low and kind.

'Yes, thanks. Keeping busy and having a good time.'

'So, you're not missing the glorious summer of Scotland?'

She giggled. 'Hardly. Mum said they had sleet last week and they're having to light the fire almost every evening. Probably similar temperatures to here actu-ally—and this is winter.'

He smiled before shovelling an enormous piece of chicken into his mouth. She relaxed, his calm presence reassuring her he was the same as she was—an over-seas visitor, albeit one with family ties.

Between bites, Sam asked Sophie about her life in

Scotland, her career as a veterinary nurse, and her travel plans for the future. Peppering her answers with questions about his own life and aspirations, the time passed quickly and Sophie felt a pang of regret when he stood and picked up his plate.

'I'm sorry I have to get back to the bar, Sophie. It's been great having the chance to chat.'

Part of her wanted him to ask when they could catch up again, while a little voice niggled inside her head, reminding her he was in a relationship with Ciara and was just being polite.

She let out a quiet breath as she watched him walk away, a wave of loneliness washing over her. The talk of home had brought memories flooding back—of the hills around their village coloured purple with heather and, in the winter, lying in a warm bath listening to music while the owl living in the tree outside the window gave a mournful call.

Despite being in the warm embrace of the Shepherd family and her brother, she choked back the tear of homesickness that threatened to roll down her cheek.

20

Finding Ciara busy serving a couple when he returned, Sam busied himself stacking the empty glasses, taking them to the kitchen, and filling the dishwasher. He couldn't stop thinking about Sophie. Gentle and quiet, her freckled nose perfectly complimented her auburn hair and open and friendly expressions. The complete opposite of his girlfriend.

Returning to the bar, he glanced at Ciara. Engaged with the man ordering the drinks, her immaculate makeup and bright persona oozed confidence and charm.

Since finding the blue wallet, suspicion had haunted him and the attraction that had burned for her had waned. He didn't consider himself a flirt and, although he had enjoyed a few brief relationships in the past, until meeting Ciara, the only love he'd experienced had been for his family and pets. Humiliation stabbed. Had he made a fool of himself? Or worse— had Ciara made a fool of him?

As though understanding his need for a distraction, a group of locals entered the bar, their voices raised with happiness and banter.

Recognising the school principal, Quinn, his wife, Joanne, and Damian and Ashleigh, who were Friday night regulars, he reached for the glasses in anticipation of their order.

'When are you going to have a hit of tennis with us?' Quinn slid onto a bar stool, his small, athletic frame in defiance of the grey hairs that peppered his dark mop, suggesting he was not as young as Sam had first thought.

When Sam and Ciara had met them during the first week of being in the village, he had discussed playing doubles with Quinn, Joanne, and Claire, and had promised to join their regular tennis nights when he could. However, Ciara hadn't been keen, professing she didn't like tennis and there were better things to do with their spare time.

Dismissing the memory, Sam shrugged. 'Hopefully soon. We've almost finished the improvements here and have been assured by Briony we'll settle into a normal work routine as soon as the big opening night is behind us.'

'Good to hear.' Quinn nodded toward the glass and

bottle of Cascade Light beer Sam held in his hand. 'Yep. You've got it, mate.'

With Ciara and most other patrons having drifted into the dining room or settled in a corner, Sam enjoyed an uninterrupted half hour with the friendly group clustered around the bar. Featherwood Falls may be small, but except for the occasional work-worn and lonely local who came more for the opportunity to air their grievances than drink, Sam had found the patrons welcoming and inclusive.

Perhaps that's why Ciara seems keen to stay longer than we originally thought?

The evening drifted on, the tennis group moving to the dining room while others wandered off home. Ciara hadn't returned from her tea break but with surprise, Sam realised her absence didn't worry him one bit. Instead, unease lodged deep inside him, gnawing over the passports, and he questioned himself for the umpteenth time. He needed to discuss it with someone—but who? He didn't dare ask Ciara. Not only could that create a tantrum, but if she was doing something illegal, he didn't want to be a part of it—and he knew better than most how manipulative and convincing she could be. Was it legal to have two passports in different names? He suspected not. Why then did she have them?

His head spun as Rhys and James led the Shepherd

women, Sophie, and Kirk into the hotel lobby. Sophie lifted her hand in a tiny wave as they passed.

Such an open and honest face, he thought, lifting a hand in return. A vision of Ciara hovered as Sophie disappeared through the door. Complications were not in his vocabulary, but the difference between the two young women new to this town couldn't be more obvious.

Wracked with fear and self-doubt, he furiously sprayed and wiped the tables, thrust trays of glassware into the dishwasher, and restocked the shelves behind the bar, pausing only to farewell the departing customers with a hand-raise and word of thanks.

Briony entered the room at the exact moment a fleeting thought of packing his gear and doing a runner crossed his mind, her face solemn and her shoulders slumped. He paused, swallowed his thoughts, and shot her a friendly smile.

There is no way I'm leaving this place with my work unfinished. And there's no way I will let you and Alex down.

BRIONY WIPED HER FOREHEAD, leaving a sooty streak across one flushed cheek. Winter had arrived and as each day passed, frosts hardened the ground a little more while trees released the last of their autumn colours.

'What's up, lass?' Alex frowned at the blackened pile of paper in the ancient fire grate.

'I'm trying to light this damn fire, that's what!' she snapped.

He rested a hand on her shoulder and gently eased her aside. 'Let me have a go.'

Grasping the poker from the hearth, he squatted and rearranged what was left of the wads of paper and a handful of twigs. Then, with years of practiced expertise, he made fresh twists of the old newspaper and lay it in the grate, criss-crossing the twigs over them before balancing a further tee-pee of wooden kindling sticks on top. One flick of the lighter and the flames grew into a perfect tent of bright orange.

Alex stood and reached for three larger pieces of wood, fed the fire, and turned to hug Briony. 'You'll be right now, love. You're just out of practice. Why didn't you leave it to me or Sam—like every other day?'

Briony rubbed her upper arms with open palms. 'Our first paying guest arrives today, and I wanted the entire building to be nice and warm to welcome her.'

Alex glanced at the clock on the wall. 'It's not even seven o'clock yet. Didn't you say she'd be here around lunchtime?'

'Yeah, well, I know how long it takes for these

rooms to warm up properly. And there's nothing like a friendly fire that's been burning for hours.'

He grinned and squeezed her again. 'Why don't you put the heating on for a while until the fire gets going. They'll take the chill off the place while we have breakfast.'

Grudgingly, Briony switched on the new, wall-mounted reverse-cycle air-conditioning systems. Having insulation pumped into the ceiling space of the old building and replacing dangerously old electric heaters had made a significant difference to their heating bill, but Briony was determined to reduce the overheads further and had spent hours mulling over the eye-watering quotes for installing solar panels on the roof. *After the official opening. When custom builds up and the income exceeds expenses.*

Moving to the dining room, Briony emulated Alex's fire-lighting process, pausing to admire the beautiful porcelain tiles edging either side and along the top beneath the mantlepiece.

By eleven o'clock, Briony peeped through the front windows at every opportunity, looking out for their guest. The upstairs room had been prepared the previous day—Briony had wiped the interior of the old timber wardrobe with a lavender-oiled cloth, polished the windows facing the back of the hotel where mowed grass ran down to the stream until they sparkled, and tweaked the floral quilt and curtains until every crease was smoothed out. A vase of camelias from Ginny's garden sat on the dressing table with a small crystal bowl and ring holder perfectly placed on the matching lace doilies at either end of the tabletop. Everything was exactly as they had been in Briony's grandmother's home before she had passed away suddenly a year earlier.

'There. That should make a more mature woman feel at home,' Briony had said aloud when she'd finished, despite being the only person in the room.

Certain her efforts would be appreciated, she returned to the window and glanced up the road for the hundredth time.

AT EXACTLY TWELVE NOON, a tiny grey car crept down the main street before halting outside the hotel. After turning slowly into the car park, it came to a stop and a woman stepped out wearing a burgundy-coloured cloche hat and a matching coat.

Briony hurried along the hallway, calling toward the kitchen, 'Our guest is here. I'll help her with her bags.' Then she sped through the front door and along the paved pathway at the side of the building.

'Hello! Mrs Worth?'

Standing tall and straight, the woman took a step away from the car, her pale, wrinkled face creasing into a smile. 'Hello. And yes, it is.' She held out her hand. 'Eleanor Worth.'

Briony grasped it, surprised at the strength of the bony fingers. 'Welcome to Featherwood Falls Hotel. How was your trip? Did you have any trouble finding us?' she gabbled, attempting to contain her excitement.

'A little tiring and no, finding my way was easy. I studied the map before I left home and followed the instructions my phone gave me.'

'Wonderful. Let me help you with your bags. I'm sure you're looking forward to a nice cup of tea?'

Eleanor nodded, popping the car boot open with the push of a button on her key ring. 'Tea would be lovely, thank you.'

Having led the way inside, Briony paused in the entrance, relieved the warmth had filtered through the building. She admired the potted mandarin tree, an extra welcome laden with fruit and standing in a tub in the corner where it gave the place an air of historical grandeur. 'Shall we do the paperwork and get you something to eat and drink before I show you to your room?'

'Thank you. That's very kind.' After removing her hat and unbuttoning her coat, Mrs Worth dipped her head slightly, stroking loose grey hairs back into the thick French knot running down the back of her skull.

Briony's eyes widened. Eleanor Worth wasn't what she had expected, but now she wasn't sure what that had been. A shabbily dressed woman of minimal means? A wealthy retiree? The woman in front of her appeared to be neither. Comfortably dressed, Eleanor's clothing gave away nothing. Her cashmere jumper and silk scarf were of good quality but well-worn. Briony dropped her glance to Mrs Worth's shoes—her grandmother had always said you could tell what sort of person a stranger was by their shoes. Clean and polished, shabby and comfortable, or just plain grotty—the state of footwear gave a mostly accurate assessment of the wearer's personality.

Briony's intrigue grew. The black brogues were clean and polished but the leather cracked and worn. She smiled at Mrs Worth. Dismissing her grandmother's method of categorising people, Briony looked forward to getting to know this woman and was sure she would fit into Featherwood Falls nicely.

21

‘That was a wonderfully restorative pot of tea, Briony. And lunch was perfect—enough to fill the gap but not leave me feeling uncomfortable. Thank you.'

Eleanor dabbed her lips with the napkin as Briony collected the plates, an amused quiver twitching her mouth. In this old dining room, with its fragrances of lemon-scented wood polish and mouth-watering food, Briony imagined herself a hundred years earlier serving a well-heeled duchess. The only thing missing was her black dress, frilly apron, and cap.

‘I shall unpack and take a rest before joining Frank, Lola, and Zoe for dinner at their home this evening,' Eleanor added. ‘It is such a relief knowing how happy Zoe is here and that the Brown family has given her a home she truly deserves. I believe your cousin Andrew has also become a good friend to Zoe.' She paused for a moment, a fleeting sadness in her eyes. 'Poor child had a tough few years before her mother died. I know she's only one of many teenaged girls who go through hell, but despite the tragic circumstances, it pleases me she's been given a second chance.'

Briony wasn't sure what to say. She didn't know Zoe well, but agreed she deserved a wonderful home and, from what she had seen so far, seemed happy and surprisingly mature for her age. 'She's a lovely girl. Lola and Frank adore her—and from what I've heard, so do her father and stepmother.'

'Oh yes. She speaks highly of Emma and is very excited about having a little brother in a few months.'

Briony grinned. 'Everyone is, I think. This baby will be very welcome and loved. You mentioned Andrew, but I'm not sure you will meet him on this trip as he's overseas—on a tour of Europe with a farming group. I believe they're exploring various methods of growing vegetables.'

Eleanor's eyes widened with interest, and they chatted for a further few minutes. Then she excused herself and retreated upstairs.

IT WAS after nine that night when Frank, Lola, and Zoe escorted her back to the hotel, entering the almost empty bar room as Briony was polishing the countertops.

'Hello there.' She dropped her cloth and walked toward them, smiling at their guest. 'How was your evening, Mrs Worth?'

'Lovely, thank you. And please, call me Eleanor.'

Out of the corner of her eye, Briony caught Zoe's surprised expression. The little she had gleaned from Lola about the woman before today was only that she had been a neighbour of Zoe and her mother and had cared for Zoe on occasions when her mother had been out or delayed due to work. Neither Lola nor Zoe had known Mrs Worth's first name until Briony took the room reservation. And now the first meeting between them had taken place—no doubt accompanied by a delicious meal from Lola and a warm welcome from them all.

Eleanor's cheeks pinked as she tugged her scarf off and shrugged out of her coat.

'Let me take that for you ... Eleanor,' Briony said. 'Would any of you like a drink? Or a cup of tea?'

Lola cast a quick glance around at her companions as Briony waited.

After headshakes and murmurs, Mrs Worth elaborated. 'Thank you for a wonderful evening. It's been a long day and I'm ready for bed.'

Lola clasped Eleanor's hands between her own. 'Of course. You have a good sleep and tomorrow, after

Zoe's gone to school, Frank and I will pick you up and take you for a tour of the area.'

Alex entered the room, wiping his hands on a towel. 'I believe a team is coming from Warwick in the morning to begin with the enquiries and DNA collection about the baby's death. Do you need to share anything with them?'

'No. We didn't have family living in the area back then ... and we hadn't even been born!' Lola exploded with laughter.

Alex chuckled, clearly failing to notice Eleanor's surprised expression at the suggestion of DNA. 'That's grand,' he said.

'I suppose we should pop into the police station before we get busy here.' Briony grimaced. 'Not much point in Mum going because it's Dad's heritage in question, not Mum's.'

'Do what you think is right, love.' Lola shot Briony an understanding smile. 'I'm sure it will have nothing to do with your family, but every little bit of help from us will hopefully complete the puzzle.'

'Yeah.' Briony gave Lola a quick hug. 'You'd better get home now before you get cold.'

While Zoe locked elbows with Lola, Frank reached out and grasped his wife's gloved hand. 'There's not a cloud in the sky tonight, so it'll be another chilly one,' he said cheerfully.

'And I admit I am looking forward to seeing frost

again. I haven't experienced temperatures this cold for many years.' Eleanor's voice took on a soft and dreamy tone as she spoke.

'Well, unless you want to risk chilblains and slipping on the icy footpath, I'd suggest you stay in bed until the sun is well and truly up,' Frank retorted with a chuckle.

They all laughed before Eleanor headed for the stairs, and Briony and Alex waved the others goodbye, pausing on the footpath to study the sky.

In the cold, still air, Frank, Lola, and Zoe's voices slowly faded, their frames shadowed in silver as a full moon beamed down.

'What a gorgeous night.' Briony's voice was barely a whisper.

'Just like on the Isle of Skye,' Alex said, turning to face Briony.

As their eyes met, they both smiled, knowing the other was remembering the first time they had kissed —on a night exactly like this one almost four years earlier.

Alex slid his arm over her shoulders as they returned inside, whispering in her ear, 'You go up now, love. I'm finished in the kitchen and Sam said he'd close up.'

Drained from her early start and mental exertion, Briony released a long, relieved breath. 'I'm going to have a soak in the bath.'

'Perfect. Make it deep because I'll be there in a few minutes.' He kissed her on the tip of her nose.

Climbing the stairs to their newly refurbished quarters, a warm flush of love and joy pulsed through her.

MIST HUNG in the valley the following morning, leaving pearls of dampness on Briony's thick hair as she and Alex walked hand in hand to the police station. A queue was already forming outside the shabby building, with people stamping their feet and calling greetings to each other with puffs of frost-laden breath. Clearly, the notice in the shopfront window had done its job. Word had spread quickly that the team taking statements and DNA samples would begin at nine that morning.

'Hi, Briony. Alex.' The deep voice boomed out of the fog.

Briony turned to see Ryan and Emma, Lola and Frank's son and his wife, approaching. Despite her knee-length quilted coat, Emma's pregnancy was obvious, and her cheeks glowed with good health and happiness.

'I love your poster,' Emma said.

Briony frowned. 'Do you mean the one in the shop about this morning?'

'No. The lovely one about "New Beginnings at Featherwood Falls Hotel". It's in the shop window too.'

Alex snorted. 'That'll be your sister, Briony. Always one step ahead of both of us.'

Briony suddenly remembered the departing wave of approval she'd given Claire as she'd been hurrying to her car with a bunch of flowers and greenery from their mother's garden days earlier. Claire had offered to design posters to put around town, and Briony had agreed while her mind swirled with thoughts of the new stove's delayed delivery and the progress of the pizza oven.

'I haven't seen it yet. We'll pop into the store before we head back. I wonder why Claire didn't drop a few off with us first?'

Ryan shot her a guilty look. 'That could have been my fault. She called in last night for milk as I was locking up. Said she was on her way home from the farm after printing the posters. I asked if I could see them, and she gave me one.' He shrugged. 'I put it in the window straight away—looks great.'

Briony exchanged a worried glance with Alex. She trusted Claire. After all, her own artistic skills were no match for Claire's, and she was sure the poster would be both beautiful and eye-catching. But the suddenness of the celebration being only four weeks away triggered panic inside her. There seemed so much to do before then—and now with the police in town taking samples and the locals swarming about excitedly, discussing both the baby mystery and the celebratory opening, she was consumed with an overwhelming desire to climb into bed and hide under the blankets.

'It will be lovely, Briony. You and I both saw the draft and admired it, so I guess Claire assumed it was good to go.' Alex nudged her with his elbow. 'Remember what we discussed about sharing the load? This is one of those occasions where outsourcing, even with family members, is a benefit, not a disadvantage.'

She shrugged and stepped forward as the queue moved closer to the police station steps.

'I hear your Irish bar attendant is popular,' Ryan said.

Alex grinned at the couple. 'We're so lucky. I can't believe she and Sam turned up when they did—right when we needed them most. And yes, Ciara is a cheerful and efficient employee. Customers love her.'

A pang of unease startled Briony. She agreed with Alex. Ciara was all of those things. But there was something about the girl that made Briony feel uncomfortable, and she couldn't work out what that was.

WITHIN THIRTY MINUTES, Briony and Alex were trudging hand in hand to the hotel. The process had been simple and quick—a swab inside the cheek, a few minutes to answer questions and sign the form, and they were thanked by the statuesque officer allocated to the process and dismissed.

'I wonder where this will lead. Rhys reckons it's a long shot, but I suppose they have to start somewhere.' Briony increased her step to keep up with Alex's long stride.

'I'm surprised they're taking it so seriously. It was a long time ago and these tests must be costing the government a packet.'

'Perhaps it's a cold case—and the police aren't saying anything?'

Alex shrugged. 'I don't think so. But they have to do their due diligence—and finding out who the child was is part of that before they can pass the history side of things over to the university or whoever does the next step.'

'Yeah, I don't think this little baby was a missing person.' She paused for a moment before continuing softly, 'I reckon she belonged to someone working or staying in our hotel—and I suspect the police think so, too.'

22

Sam patted the final coat of mortar over the pizza oven and stood back to admire his and Kirk's creation. They had studied plans and procedures online, talked to other venues who had made their own, and were confident that what they had built was everything it needed to be: a strongly constructed chimney with a large, fire-bricked cavity and thick steel plates large enough to hold six pizzas at a time.

'It looks fantastic!'

Consumed with how he should handle the Ciara passport issue and the completed project in front of him, he jumped at Briony's compliment.

'Huh? Thanks.'

'Look at what you guys have accomplished in a few weeks.' Her voice rose with excitement. 'The scruffy backyard has gone. We have a gorgeous pizza oven, fire pit, and beautifully paved outdoor entertaining area. What more could a country pub need?'

They shared a laugh as Sam gazed around. She was right. Ever since he and Ciara had moved into the staff quarters, he had struggled to keep his mind on the job. Terrified Ciara would notice his distracted behaviour, he had thrown himself into turning the huge backyard into a landscaped park. The previously tatty, burr-filled expanse of dirt was now fresh, well-watered grass. Small trees lined the boundaries, and a pretty, white-painted pergola, complete with wooden seating on two sides, sat halfway down the slope. Tubs of plants divided the tables in the outdoor beer garden, providing individuality and a hint of privacy. Kirk had put the final touches to the new facilities and now there was only the preparation for the rebirth of the hotel to deal with.

Having willingly chopped the truckload of firewood Kirk had delivered from the farm, Sam stacked it in the sturdy timber shed tucked behind the kitchen—a legacy of years passed. His final big job was to help install the new kitchen benches and shelving when they arrived. Then once the grand opening event was over, his job would be done. He and Ciara could leave. Except a part of him didn't want to. Her casual, almost dismissive attitude toward him had been irritating—a complete change from the devotion she had shown when they had first met. If he left, she would expect to go with him—and he was shocked to realise that was no longer his greatest wish.

SAM SILENCED the music with a tap of the green icon and pressed his phone against his ear, his mind miles away. 'Hello?'

'I hope you don't mind me discussing your wonderful talents behind your back—but I've been talking with Briony, and she said she can spare you to give us a hand on the farm for a few days,' Ginny said.

The unexpected opportunity to get away from the hotel without having to take Ciara made his heart leap. 'Yes. Of course. I'd love to help.'

'Great. We're bringing the sheep in for crutching next week—want to get the job done before the pub's opening and we've got heaps to do before then.'

A vision of himself bending over hundreds of merino bellies, removing the dirty wool from around their rear-ends, flashed through his mind. It wasn't something he was experienced with and helping an uncle a couple of times as a teenager hadn't provided him with any qualifications except to understand the basic layout of a woolshed and the long, tiring days of chasing sheep and filling catching pens. The task was a far cry from his skills, and he grimaced. 'So ... how can I help?'

'The yards need maintenance. Most of the old timber railings should be replaced before we bring the sheep in or we're likely to have them crashing through barriers and escaping all over the place.'

He paused before answering, wondering if he was expected to do the job alone.

As though reading his mind, Ginny continued, 'Kirk and Sophie will both be helping, of course. And me.'

'Okay, sure. When do you want me to come?'

'Tomorrow? Briony said she and Alex can manage with Ciara's help for a week or two. If we can get this done, including the crutching, we'll all be free to help for the few days before the hotel function.'

'Yeah, no worries, Ginny. See you at … seven?'

'Sounds perfect. Thanks, Sam.'

He let his shoulders sag with relief. Deferring a tough decision wasn't the best idea, but time spent away from Ciara might be just what he needed to sort out his scrambled thoughts and put a plan in place. A comforting happiness flickered through him again, wiping away the doubts and questions that had been festering.

SOPHIE SHOVELLED the dirt away from the hole Sam had created with the fence post auger, her earnest face catching his eye. Kirk had marked out the plan with spray paint as he and Ginny had modified the current yard design and now, while Sam operated the post-hole digger, Kirk levered the key posts into place using the excavator on the back of the tractor.

A weak winter sun chased the chilly breeze away as they worked, and by the time they stopped to enjoy Ginny's fresh scones and tea at ten o'clock, Sam had shed two layers of clothes and rolled up the sleeves of his flannelette shirt.

'I'm surprised it took you this long,' Sophie said with a cheeky grin.

'I'm not as tough as you Scots. I suppose you'd call this morning's temperature summer?'

'Och, no. Our summers can get warm—and our winters are nothing like this.' She paused, tilting her head slightly as she thanked Ginny and picked up a scone. 'If I was at home, I'd call today a glorious spring —or autumn day.'

Chuckling, Sam accepted the enamel mug brimming with strong, black tea from Ginny and sat on the ramp leading into the woolshed.

'You're making good progress,' Ginny said. 'I was worried we'd be running in to crutching week before everything was done—not to mention the approaching school holidays.'

Kirk gave her a quick kiss as he reached for his mug. 'If the weather keeps on like this, the three of us will have no trouble finishing the job within the week —including the spreading of that load of gravel you've ordered.' He tipped his head back and studied the sky. 'I know we can't always rely on the weather bureau, but I reckon we'll be lucky to get rain within the next month.'

'I hope you're right. Both cabins are booked out for the holidays and while the family I'm putting in Dandelion Cabin are hoping for snow, I doubt they'll be pleased if it pours with rain.'

'Who's booked into Lavender Cabin?' Sophie asked.

'A couple from Townsville. Apparently, they're in the Defence Force and in need of a break from the heat. She grew up in Tasmania.'

'What on earth is bringing them to little Featherwood Falls?' Kirk grunted.

Ginny shrugged. 'I'm not sure, but they said they saw the advertisement for here in one of the holiday magazines Claire's been doing some marketing material for. Maybe she's from a farm and is feeling homesick, or maybe they just liked the photos Claire took—and the price. Whatever their reason, it works for me.'

'Well, good to know something's working. Claire's certainly put some hours into promoting both the pub and our farm-stay facilities—and I'm glad we changed the shearer's quarters last year. Much better having it set up as two cabins instead of just rooms with the kitchen at one end and the bathroom at the other.'

Kirk swilled the last of his tea and swallowed it with one gulp. 'I wouldn't be too keen on having to walk down an outside veranda to get to the loo on a cold winter's night and I bet our city-bred guests wouldn't either.' He chuckled as he picked up a cream-and jam-laden scone and popped it in his mouth whole. 'Better get back to it,' he mumbled.

Both Sam and Sophie handed their mugs to Ginny and thanked her before returning to the tractor.

Sam manoeuvred the vehicle according to Sophie's hand signals, backing up until the drill was precisely positioned over Kirk's yellow cross. As he lowered the auger, Sam's thoughts were once again fastened on Sophie. It had been such a simple morning—not in labour so much as ease of company. Instead of having to think about every word he said in case it upset her or sparked an argument like it did with Ciara, he and Sophie had worked tirelessly, sharing amusing quips and the occasional comment about work they'd both experienced in the past. She had been fascinated to hear about his hometown of Dargaville in New Zealand's north, and nothing was strained, upsetting, or controversial. In between bouts of conversation, they worked in companionable silence. Uncompli-cated, he told himself. Sam's tension eased—and the day passed in a productive flash.

He had said goodbye to them all, his gaze lingering a little too long on Sophie, and was about to hop in his ute to head back to the hotel when his phone rang. He jumped—his mind still metres away with his work-mate—glanced at the screen, and hesitated. "Private Number" showed. When that happened, it was usually a telemarketing call and he'd let it go to message bank. But this time, something made him swipe the green icon.

'Hello?'

'Gidday, mate.'

Sam recognised Rhys's voice and let his shoulders drop. 'Gidday. What's up?'

'Feel like a hit of tennis?'

Sam blinked. It wasn't the first time Rhys had invited him to play and he'd had to refuse because Ciara didn't want him to leave her at the pub. However, she'd be busy this evening as it was cards night, and the bar would be humming between seven and nine. He had planned to do his washing and, after dinner, lie on the bed and begin reading the latest Neil Lancaster crime thriller. He grinned to himself. That could wait. A hit of tennis would be a great way to finish an enjoyable day, even if his back suggested otherwise.

'Sure. Sounds good. What time?'

'How about straight away? I'm locking up here now and Claire won't be home until after seven. She's finishing the promos for the pub opening.'

'Okay. Give me twenty minutes to get into town and change my clothes. I'll see you at the courts.' Pierced with a sudden stab of nervous guilt, he rubbed his chin. Would this evening provide the opportunity to share the dual passport discovery? He sucked in a deep breath, his gut swirling with sickening indecision and the need to talk his concerns over with someone.

As he drove down the main street past the police station, he decided. That someone would be Rhys.

---

23

*S*am hit the ball with ferocity, returning Rhys's powerful forehands with a strength he rarely used. Tennis was not his favourite sport, but five years at a New Zealand high school had provided him with an excellent overview of many activities. He'd enjoyed tennis but in his final two years had switched to playing cricket during the summer months and rugby through winter. Since completing his education, working alongside his father with cricket as his outlet, little time had been spared to think about women, let alone date them.

He lifted his arm and served, groaning as it went wide and bounced outside the court.

'That's game, set, and match.' Rhys walked toward him with an extended hand.

Sam took it before wiping his forehead on the

sleeve of his T-shirt. 'Yeah. I know. You deserved to win.'

As they ambled back to the tennis pavilion everyone lovingly called "The Shed", Sam's thoughts swung to Ciara. How could he broach the subject with Rhys? His insides knotted. He would have to blurt something or Rhys would head home and the only thing he would have achieved was to have lost a hard-fought game of tennis.

'How's Ciara? Haven't seen her outside the pub for weeks.'

Sam swung his head toward his companion so fast it jarred his neck. 'Umm. Actually ... would you mind if we had a quick talk?' He glanced around them. No sign of life except a man chopping wood in his backyard several houses away. 'Here would be good—where we can be sure of privacy.'

'Sure.' Rhys spoke slowly, his eyes narrowing. 'Is something worrying you?'

Sam took a deep breath and began. 'I'm probably overreacting and have got the wrong end of the stick ... but I wouldn't mind a second opinion if that's okay?'

'Of course. Fire away.'

Sam began with Ciara asking him—no—ordering him to pack both their gear and move into the reno-vated bedroom downstairs.

Rhys's attention never wavered, his eyes fixed on Sam's as he continued, sharing the discovery of the money—and the passports with all the information they held.

'Have you got the photos of the passports and cards with you?'

Sam picked up his jacket from the bench seat and pulled his phone from the pocket. He scrolled through to the photos and then passed the device to Rhys.

A slow whistle blew through Rhys's lips as he studied it. After handing the phone back to Sam, he grunted quietly. 'This is highly unusual. Why is Naomi using Ciara's name? The photos look very similar, but they are two different people.' Pausing, as though uncertain of Sam's reaction to his next comment, Rhys rubbed a hand through his hair. 'I don't think you're being over-reactive at all. In fact, I think you've got evidence of something not being quite right.'

'So, what should I do?'

'Send me those photos, if you don't mind.'

'Okay. Email or text?'

'Email. They'll come through at a higher definition.' Rhys shared his email address, and they both watched as Sam attached the photos and hit send. After waiting for what seemed like minutes but was only a few seconds, Rhys nodded. 'Got them.' His eyes narrowed. 'Is she using drugs?'

Sam's jaw dropped as he stood speechless for a long minute. 'I don't think so—but I wouldn't know.

Haven't had much to do with the stuff myself. Why do you ask?'

'Her disappearance in Melbourne could account for the purchase and use of a substance or two—and the wad of cash. She may have been on a bender.' He paused and took a deep breath. 'You also mentioned she has mood swings—which I know is common for some people—but whenever I've seen her in the hotel, she's been bright and bubbly. Could be she's not getting a chance to use regularly. And that can make a person cranky and unreasonable. And if she is using something, she obviously doesn't want you to know which could mean she experiences withdrawal symptoms before she can sneak her next hit—or snort.'

'Good grief.' Sam rubbed a hand through his hair. 'I never thought about it—but I have noticed her eyes change sometimes—and now I think about it, it's usually when she's at her most flirtatious and outgoing.' He stared at Rhys with bulging eyes. 'What will you do?'

'First, I'll have a chat with James. He's the detective you met when you discovered the baby's body. We've worked together for a few years now and he's a good bloke. Regardless of the potential drug suspicion, I expect he'll want to get Interpol involved immediately —to check if either of those women's names are on the missing-persons list, both here in Australia and overseas.'

'Jeez. You think this could be something more serious that just having picked up a friend's passport then?'

'Yes. I do. Why otherwise would someone have two passports from different countries with similar-looking photos but a different name—not to mention the bank and sim cards.'

Sam nodded. That had been exactly his concern from the moment he had seen them. 'You're right. Then what happens?'

'Well, we'll wait until we find out if someone is missing. If not, my guess is that James will call Ciara in for a chat ... just to see what she has to say.'

'And if you do that, she will know straight away that I found them and have reported her.' He grimaced as his shoulders sagged. 'I can't see that ending well for me.'

Rhys rested a hand on Sam's shoulder. 'Hey, mate. Don't worry about it. I'll give James a call when I get back to the station and I'll let you know what he says— with no one else knowing a thing. One step at a time. Trust me.'

The weight that had been sitting on Sam for weeks began to lift, and he smiled. 'Thanks, Rhys. I will.'

With the subject jamming his mind with doubt and suspicion, Sam gathered his gear and strode along the road beside Rhys, sharing an understanding nod of thanks outside the police station and continuing to the hotel.

SOPHIE LAY ON HER BACK, her hands behind her head as she stared at the ceiling. Despite hours having passed since she waved Sam goodbye, she couldn't get him out of her mind.

He's in a relationship. Stop thinking about him.

Rolling over, she pulled the pillow against her ear. Her self-chiding wasn't working. Of course he had a girlfriend. He was the nicest guy she'd met in years and working with him had reminded her that not all males were like Peter. She scowled into the dark. Ciara was lucky to have Sam in her life. A vision of the Irish girl sprang to mind—no matter how often she mentally revisited the party, she was sure the Ciara in Featherwood Falls was the person she'd met in Inverness.

Angst rolled in her gut, stealing her breath. Except for the week of painting, she had been to the Featherwood Falls pub only twice. But each time she had studied Ciara as subtly as she could, her thoughts racing until she felt dizzy with exertion.

I've heard it said that we all have a double somewhere on earth; perhaps Ciara's lives in Scotland.

Determinedly, she forced her thoughts to the following day's chores. School holidays were looming, and the horses needed to be well-groomed, in good condition, and ready to give Claire's pupils and the farm-stay children endless rides. It had become a habit for Sophie to rise early and take the dogs for a run before breakfast before bringing the horses in for a quick brush and feed. Despite their planned early start with the yards, she would not let Ginny or the men down. She would have her jobs completed and be waiting at the woolshed when Sam arrived.

With her plan fixed firmly in her mind, she focused on her breathing, allowing her body to relax, and drifted into sleep.

24

---

*B*riony dragged herself out of bed and staggered into the shower. It had been an exhausting two months and the financial burden of restoring the hotel to a fresh and welcoming hostelry was weighing heavily on her. She envied Alex's ability to whistle and sing as he worked, content in the knowledge he could concoct his choice of meals and not have to answer to the hierarchy. It was Briony who worried for both of them.

What will happen when the bank loan reaches its maximum—when every dollar has been allocated and spent?

Despite the increasing popularity of Alex's meals and the steady stream of both locals and travellers stopping in for lunch or a drink, the profits were being gobbled up by expenses like plumbing and electricity costs that had far exceeded Briony's estimates. On top of renovation and running costs, having extra staff to pay was adding to their outlay, even if Ciara and Sam had earned every cent and proved popular with customers.

She stepped under the cascade of hot water and sighed. At least the bathrooms were functional and nice, the guest and staff bedrooms refurbished, and the outside and inside wore a fresh coat of paint where needed. While focusing on the list of improvements they had achieved, a small smile touched Briony's lips as she shampooed her hair. If it hadn't been for her mother's, Kirk's, and Sophie's help, she doubted the business would have got off to such a successful start. Squaring her shoulders, she rinsed her hair and turned off the taps. Now they needed to concentrate on the farm, and it was over to her and Alex to continue the positivity.

There was no sign of either Ciara or Sam in the kitchen. Alex looked up from where he was preparing a breakfast tray for Eleanor and grinned. 'Just you and me this morning, my lassie.'

'I'm guessing Ciara is still asleep and Sam's gone to the farm?'

'Yep. I told Ciara she didn't need to start until eleven this morning.'

Briony raised her eyebrows. After arriving home the previous evening, Sam had barely said a word while they ate dinner, and then after the bar had closed and she and Alex were doing their final kitchen clean for the day, they had heard raised voices coming from Sam and Ciara's quarters.

'Did you talk to her after we finished last night?'

'Yeah. After you went upstairs, I did my routine security round.' His voice dropped to a whisper. 'Caught her sneaking a whisky in the bar—and she hadn't written it in the book.'

Briony sucked in a breath and frowned. 'Really?' When she hired them, they'd agreed to allowing two free drinks per day, but after that, they would record whatever they consumed in a notebook and Briony would deduct the wholesale cost of the alcohol from their pay each week.'

'I let it go. She was angry, and I didn't want to make things worse.'

Briony stared at him for a moment before nodding in agreement. Since Sam and Ciara had moved downstairs, their relationship appeared to have changed. Acknowledging they were all living under the same roof and friction was bound to creep in at some point, Briony had dismissed it as a lover's tiff. However, something about Ciara still bothered her. The girl was friendly and helpful with customers and, although frequently later than Sam to start her shifts, always stayed later in the evenings to make up for it. Her Irish accent drew an increase of patrons, who lounged around the bar chatting to her. Her soft lilt sounded surprisingly Australian at times, but Briony reasoned that was to be expected when surrounded by locals for most of her day.

She moved to the coffee machine and made them both a large mugful of the fragrant elixir before plonking herself on a chair. 'It's Wednesday. Will you be okay here on your own while I pop up to the shop and collect the apple pies from Lola?'

Alex moved to sit beside her, leaned over, and kissed her on the cheek before picking up his coffee. 'Of course. We've got three families and two couples booked in for dinner tonight, plus Eleanor, so I've got plenty to keep me busy. I thought panna cotta and sticky date pudding for dessert would give enough variety with the pies—agreed?'

Briony placed a hand on his. 'You know I do. Your menus are awesome, and we haven't received a complaint yet.'

Alex rolled his eyes and plastered a horrified expression on his face. 'And what's more, I hope we never do.'

Briony stood and walked to the fridge. 'Scrambled eggs?'

'Sounds great. You make it while I prep the vegetables for soup.'

Half an hour later, with empty plates in front of them, they languished a few minutes longer than usual

—Briony relishing their companionable solitude while a family of magpies serenaded them outside the window.

THE DOORBELL tinkled as Briony entered the store.

'Hello, love. I thought you'd be in any minute.' Lola greeted Briony with a hug before stepping back and studying her briefly. 'You're still looking tired, my girl.'

Briony shrugged. She had heard it all before and sometimes wished Lola didn't know her so well. 'I am a bit—but you would know more than most about that. There's not much spare time when you're running your own business, is there? Especially a hospitality business.'

Lola nodded vigorously. 'True.' She swept her gaze around the shop before resting it on the pies sitting on the kitchen counter. 'At least now we've got Ryan home, and Janet working most days, I don't get out of bed until seven.' Laughter gurgled in her throat. 'I must admit I'm quite liking semi-retirement.'

Briony exploded with laughter. 'You're amazing. In your seventies and still cooking lamingtons and scones for your café, plus whatever extra desserts we need each week. Not to mention keeping up to date with the house and post office. I hope I'm as good as you are when I get to your age.'

Lola gave a dismissive wave as she turned toward the kitchen. 'Huh. You'll be fine now the renovations are finished.' She shot Briony a small frown. 'They are, aren't they?'

'Yes, thank goodness. The kitchen installation was a breeze after all my worrying, so now Sam's helping Mum and Kirk at the farm. They're crutching the wethers next week and then have farm-stay bookings. Not long now until the "Grand Opening".' She lifted both hands, imitating quotation marks with her fingers as a ripple of excitement ran through her.

'I'm looking forward to it. Do you know Eleanor told me yesterday she's thinking of staying on just to be here for the event?' Lola said.

Briony lifted an eyebrow. 'Wow. It hasn't taken her long to become one of us, has it?'

'Not at all. It's been lovely getting to know her and, of course, Zoe has enjoyed catching up again. Until I heard some stories they've shared, I hadn't realised just how often Eleanor cared for Zoe.' She paused, her eyes filled with sadness. 'That girl had some tough years and I'm eternally grateful for what Eleanor did. After all, she was simply a neigh-bour with no blood ties and no children of her own.'

'She must have been married though—otherwise I don't imagine she would call herself "Mrs"?'

Lola nodded. 'Oh yes, she mentioned her husband

died in the Vietnam War, only six weeks after they were married.'

'How awful for her. Has she been on her own all these years?'

'Yes. She was a teacher until retirement, apparently, so I guess that's where she gained such an understanding of children and teenagers. Said she has no family that she knows of, so I imagine Zoe was just as important to her as she was to Zoe.'

Briony studied her friend. Lola had been in her life longer than her own grandmother. It had been a shock to them all when Ryan discovered he had a daughter and had brought her to live in Featherwood Falls after Zoe's mother died. But according to Ginny, Lola had welcomed the sixteen-year-old into her home like a long-lost family member. Which, she reflected, was exactly what Zoe was. *I wonder how Lola really feels about meeting the woman who was like a grandmother to Zoe before she was placed in Ryan's care.*

'Eleanor said she's spending today researching her family history. Whatever you discovered yesterday apparently provided her with a renewed enthusiasm to learn something about her heritage,' Briony said.

'Yes. We visited a gorgeous little chapel and wandered through the cemetery. We met a nice chap there—a retired vicar who introduced himself as Timothy Cross. He showed us where the oldest graves were, some dating back to the eighteen seventies.

Eleanor has an interest in finding out more about her family, and he shared his phone number with her in case she would like help. Apparently, he has experience in navigating this ancestry thing.'

The door tinkled again as Rhys rushed in. 'Hello, ladies.' He paused, facing each in turn. 'Sorry, am I interrupting?'

'No. We were just chatting—you know me,' said Lola.

He chuckled. 'Any chance of a couple of your lamingtons?'

'Of course. Hang on a tick.' She popped two large chocolate and coconut-coated rectangles into a paper bag and handed them to him. 'Morning tea for you and Claire?'

Intrigue halted Briony as he hesitated for a beat.

'No. Actually, James is calling in. We've got a couple of things to discuss.'

'Any progress on the little baby?' Lola's face creased with hopeful concern.

He shook his head. 'Nothing yet, but people have been surprisingly generous in having their DNA tested, so we're hopeful something might come of that. Anyway, thanks, Lola. Catch you later.'

As he dashed out the door, Lola and Briony's eyes met. 'Hmm, something's on his mind. It's not like Rhys to be in such a rush,' Lola said.

'A busy day for him, I guess.' Briony handed Lola

the cake tray she had tucked under one arm. 'I'd better get back to the pub too or Alex will think I've abandoned him.'

Lola guffawed before passing two enormous apple pies across the counter to Briony.

The pies safely secured on the tray and covered with a clean cloth, Briony lifted them and followed Lola to the door, kissing her lightly on the cheek as she passed through. 'Thanks again. See you tomorrow?'

'Yes. We'll be there for quiz night. Can't miss that. The last one was a hoot.'

Briony grinned. When Quinn, the school principal, had suggested a quiz night to bring the community to the hotel, Briony had doubted they would ever get enough contestants to make such an event worthwhile. But she had been wrong. What had started with only eight participants had spurred interest in the town and now more than twenty had nominated for the following night's event, requesting the evening be repeated every second week. Quinn had agreed to run the competition, and neither Alex nor Briony could see why it would do anything but improve sales for them, so they had agreed and hoped the quiz brought an influx of patrons to eat and drink at their hotel.

'See you then.'

25

Sam lay on his back, listening to the regular rhythm of Ciara's breathing. Sleep eluded him, and all he could think about was his conversation with Rhys. Giving up all attempts to still his mind, he crept outside and sat on the veranda step. The night was cold and clear, the sky bright with stars and lit by a thick Milky Way against the inky background, like a bride's veil.

With elbows propped on his knees, he rested his head in his hands, forcing his concentration to the sound of the burbling creek at the bottom of the garden. While it soothed him, the regular loud rattling call from a possum in a nearby tree added to the serenade, tugging a brief smile from him before he lapsed back into a pit of guilt. Had he betrayed his girlfriend?

The thought gnawed at the lump of dread sitting in his stomach.

He closed his eyes and forced his mind away from Ciara, dwelling instead on the work remaining at Featherwood Station and the upcoming celebrations at the pub. How long could he cope with bluffing his way through being Ciara's partner? There was no partnership at all anymore. Had there ever been? *Great boyfriend I am.* He grunted, mentally punishing himself for being so gullible, so easily influenced. The words of one of Elvis Presley's songs bounced into his mind—one his father sang with gusto after a few beers at every family gathering. *Only fools rush in ...*

And I'm the fool.

Eventually, the icy air penetrated numbed thoughts and limbs. Rising stiffly, he returned to the bedroom, promising himself that as soon as the big opening night was over, he would leave Featherwood Falls—without Ciara.

BY THE END of day two at the sheep yards, the new panels were secure, the gates hung, and all that remained was to spread the load of gravel to keep the main race and area in front of the loading dock free of mud.

Ginny beamed with delight, patting both Sophie

and Sam on the back as she surveyed their labours. 'I never thought we'd achieve so much in such a brief space of time.' She glanced at her watch as Kirk approached and lay an arm over her shoulders.

'I reckon we owe these two an outing,' he said gruffly. 'For a vet nurse and a cabinet-maker, they've clocked up some brownie points as fencers and we've got at least one unexpectedly free day. How about we finish the tidying up in the morning then take a picnic up the back of the farm?' He raised his eyebrows in question as he cast his glance around.

Ginny straightened with a firm nod of approval. 'Couldn't agree more. Sam hasn't seen any of the property—not even the falls.' She beckoned. 'Come on. I could kill a cup of tea. Let's call it a day.'

A surge of happiness warmed Sam's heart and one look at Sophie's delighted face suggested she felt the same. Away from the hotel, he felt a sort of freedom. Despite the physical work, the farm provided a quieter place—one where time was slow and mellow. One where each of them could enjoy a different kind of companionship. He liked that.

'Kirk and I'll go ahead in the ute and put the kettle on. Will you two be okay to walk?'

'Of course, Ginny.' Sophie shot Sam a grin. 'Your legs are still working, aren't they?'

Chuckling, he nodded, then gathered the tools and packed them into a neat pile inside the shed door.

The afternoon sun shone in their eyes as they strolled along the track toward the house.

'Days are getting short,' Sam said.

Matching his long strides with arms swinging and a soft smile on her lips, Sophie agreed. 'Aye. But they're so beautiful here. I'm loving living in Australia, and the whole family is so kind to me …'

'I think I hear a "but"?'

'Please don't misunderstand. I'm grateful for Ginny letting me stay. I love helping and it's good getting to know Alex's Aussie family. But yes, I think once the crutching is finished and the hotel opening and school holidays are behind us, I'll be ready to move on and see what else this enormous country offers.'

'Me too.'

She turned to stare at him as they walked, her auburn hair blowing softly across her cheek.

Sam waited for the question—what about Ciara—but it didn't come. Instead, a flash of understanding crossed her face as they strode silently on.

She knew. Sam let his shoulders sag as a profound sense of relief washed over him, like the wake of a slow boat. Although no one but Rhys knew about the hidden passports or money, it was all he could do to not share his worries with this intuitive Scotswoman. She was what those from her homeland called "canny".

ON A HILL in the top-most paddock before pasture morphed to native bush, they sat around a food-laden rug on the ground. Kirk leaned back on one elbow, long legs stretched out and his wide-brimmed hat low on his forehead.

'Not a bad restaurant, is it?' He flapped a hand toward the valley in front of them. 'Great view and the tucker's not bad either.'

A small giggle burst from Sophie. She reached for an apple, rubbed it on her shirt-front and took a noisy bite. 'It's absolutely beautiful. Different to home, but just as breathtaking in a less rugged way.'

'I'd like to see Scotland.' Sam's tone was thoughtful. 'I reckon all that "Outlander" stuff on the telly must have brought a lot of interest to the country.' He glanced enquiringly at Sophie.

'It has. They even do tours of the area and they're always full. And now they've improved the coast road around the top half of our country, in summer it's bursting with holiday makers. They call the route the NC500.'

'Perhaps I should get a push bike over there and have a look at it? Cheap to run and those hills would keep me fit.'

Sophie laughed at Sam's comment. 'That could be the understatement of the year.'

'How about we head for home now and call in at the falls on the way?' Ginny said as she pushed herself to her feet and began gathering the remnants of the picnic.

Agreed murmuring signalled action, although the men both took their time to get to their feet.

'What's the plan for crutching, Ginny? Do you need my help?' Sam's voice rose hopefully. The alternative for him was remaining at the pub and working with Ciara—and since speaking to Rhys, that option was no longer one he cared for.

'Well,' Ginny began briskly. 'Claire has said she's free for a couple of days, so I thought if she and Sophie mustered the sheep, gave a hand in the yards, and then returned them to the paddocks afterwards'—she looked at Sam—'you and Kirk could do the shed work and I'll provide the meals. Sound okay?'

'Sure.'

Kirk gave Sam an understanding grin. 'That means you and I keep the inside pens full for the shearers and sweep the dirty wool and locks away, so the board remains clean for them.'

Confusion crossed both Sam's and Sophie's faces at the unfamiliar terminology, and Kirk hastily explained.

'During crutching, it's not only the dirty wool around the sheep's backsides that is removed, but also the short, often grass or weed-infested bits from around their faces and on the top of their heads. As they graze, especially if the grass is long, stalks and stuff can get stuck in the wool, which can also partially cover their eyes, so it's a good chance to clean that area up.'

Sam nodded. 'Good to know.'

'So, yours and my jobs also involve removing the clippings from the floor and sorting them into bins—one for the face bit we call "locks" and the other for crutchings. When the bales are sold, Ginny won't get as much money as she gets for their fleeces, but the process is all about animal hygiene and getting rid of the dirty stuff so that when they do a full shear in spring, the wool is relatively clean.'

'What do you mean by the board?' Sophie asked.

'It's the term we use for the section of floor on which the sheep are shorn.' Ginny smiled as she spoke. 'Don't worry. We'll be there to guide you both.'

'A word of warning,' Kirk chortled.

Both Sophie and Sam fixed their eyes on him.

'Those shearers will keep you dancing—and I don't mean to music. They work fast and sometimes you'll be running to keep up with them.' He chortled. 'By the end of the day, you'll think you've done a half marathon.'

Sophie's eyes widened as she turned to face Sam. 'I think they're challenging us.'

'Yeah—but we've got youth on our side and anyway, I don't mind a challenge,' he quipped.

Sam and Sophie climbed into the back of the ute, stowing the gear beside them before positioning themselves side by side on the folded tarpaulin with their backs to the cab.

A challenge, Sam thought to himself as Kirk turned on the ignition. *I'm getting used to those.*

AFTER LEAVING the vehicle beside the cattle yards, the four of them followed the narrow track over the hill on the opposite side of the farm. As the land fell away and the homestead and southern end of the farm disappeared behind the crest of the hill, they crossed more smaller ridges before the sound of water reached them.

Leading the way, Ginny waved an arm upwards and called over her shoulder. 'At the top there's a spring. It's all granite country and water collects there in small lakes during the wet weather, then filters down the slopes until it reaches the village and flows on to join the river.'

'Where are the falls?' Sam asked.

Ginny held her arm straight out from her body as though to prevent the others from passing her. 'Stop and listen.'

They all halted silently. A family of magpies

warbled from a branch nearby and the bellow of a cow echoed through the air. A soft hissing reached them, mixed with the rumble of water over rocks in the distance, a clump of native bush muffling the sound.

'I hear it,' Sam said. 'Lead on.'

Within minutes, they reached a stand of eucalypts before winding their way through the thickening bush and reaching a flat, open area where a cluster of ancient rainforest trees filtered the water from above before it cascaded over rocks and into a circular pond. On the bottom side of the water, a jigsaw of multi-sized rocks formed a solid wall, encasing an idyllic natural pool, and beyond that, the overflow continued down the slope and along the bottom boundary of Feather-wood Station before reaching the village.

Unimpeded, the vista guided the observer's gaze into the multi-coloured valley with its orchards, crops, and network of paddocks, to the roofs of the store, police station, school, and houses before it continued up the other side into a range of bush-clad hills and rugged, ancient mountains.

'Wow. This is stunning.' Sam stood mesmerised, his hands hanging loosely at his sides.

'Yeah. We're very lucky,' Ginny murmured. 'When Lyndon and I married, the pool wasn't here. We built it gradually over years so we could have our own private paradise. Of course, it's not swimming weather now but in the summer it's a beautiful spot to come to.'

Sophie stood beside Sam, their hands almost touching as they breathed in the fresh, country air and drank in the view. 'It's absolutely perfect,' she murmured.

Sam's face wore an awe-inspired smile. 'It's a shame I won't be here for summer to try it out.'

Wordlessly, she nodded as a pang of regret filled her. She couldn't agree more.

26

―――――

Too busy for the next few days to think
about Ciara, Sam revelled in the fast-paced
work, adjusting to the smell of lanolin and sheep
manure, while the noises of the shearing plant and
bleating sheep blocked out all other sounds.

Outside, he glimpsed the girls bringing in flocks of
wethers, filling the yards, and then collecting the
finished mob from the pens behind the shed and
returning them to the respective paddocks.

In their breaks, the workers moved to the opposite
end of the shed where Ginny laid out a spread fit for
hungry helpers. Scones, sandwiches, and slices,
savouries and fruit appeared at nine-thirty and again at
three in the afternoon with a hot meal served at
midday. Sam relished every mouthful, conceding that
living and working with the Shepherd women

certainly provided a tastier diet than when picking grapes—although that too had provided benefits.

With darkness approaching, they finished at five-thirty when the shearers, a small group of men who lived within daily driving distance, returned to their homes, leaving the Featherwood Station crew sorting out sheep, cleaning and preparing the shed for the following day, and eventually dragging their weary bodies to the house for another of Ginny's sustaining meals.

By the time Sam reached the hotel each evening, he was too tired to do any more than shower and fall into bed.

ON THE LAST day in the woolshed, a Friday, the last sheep passed through the tiny door leading to the "finished" pen earlier than expected. As the Featherwood Station team completed the day's work before dark, Kirk suggested they head to the hotel for dinner with Briony and Alex.

Sam strode through the back door, grabbed a clean set of clothes, and locked himself in the bathroom for ten long minutes before emerging smelling of shampoo and a wood-scented aftershave. With his curly hair dripping into the cotton shoulders of his shirt, he gave it another rub dry and hung the towel on the rail in their bedroom before wandering into the kitchen.

Halting abruptly as he met Briony's pale face, his glance swung to Alex. Ice filled his veins as he met the chef's shocked pallor. A quiet bubbling sound coming from the stovetop filled the otherwise silent room.

'What's happened?'

Briony and Alex looked briefly at each other before Briony spoke. 'Sit down, Sam.'

He pulled out a chair and plonked himself heavily into it, his gaze fixed on Briony's as his head spun dizzily. It had to be about Ciara.

'Rhys called in.' Briony's voice was soft with disbelief and empathy. 'Said he and James needed to speak with Ciara. They went out the back for a few minutes then left, taking Ciara with them.'

A deep, rumbling groan crawled from Sam's throat. Rhys must have heard from Interpol—or perhaps he hadn't, but someone higher up had and they'd needed more information?

Gritting his teeth, all remaining energy evaporated, leaving him as deflated as a helium balloon caught on a barbed-wire fence. It was as he had feared—only worse. If they had taken her away to question, there mustn't have been a simple explanation for the two passports.

He felt a gentle hand on his shoulder. 'Are you alright, Sam?'

He looked into Briony's troubled hazel eyes and shook his head. 'I knew something wasn't right—I just didn't know what it was. I tried to get through to her that a problem shared was a problem halved but she wouldn't have a bar of it and our discussion erupted into a shouting match.'

'You mean with Ciara? Can you tell us?' Briony's understanding gaze finally penetrated Sam's conscience.

As he stared at her, he chided himself. If Rhys and Ciara had left without saying anything, Alex and Briony wouldn't know why she'd gone with Rhys. Unwilling to mention the passports, he shrugged helplessly. 'How long ago did they leave?'

'About thirty minutes.' Briony frowned. 'I'd better get into the bar. There's no one else and we've got fifteen booked in for dinner, not including us or Eleanor.'

Reality crept slowly back to Sam as the anxiety in Briony's voice registered. He pushed himself upright and drew a deep breath. 'I'll do the bar, Briony. You and Alex worry about dinner.' Then, without waiting for them to respond, he walked toward the door.

Neither she nor Alex deserved this.

There was still no sign of Ciara an hour later when Ginny, Kirk, Sophie, and Claire arrived. Claire was the first to approach the bar, sliding herself onto a stool. 'Good thing you're versatile, Sam. One minute you're a roustabout cleaning up the wool-shed and the next you're serving drinks in the poshest pub in Featherwood Falls.' She glanced around the room. 'Ciara off getting herself ready for dinner?'

'No.' He leaned forward, whispering even though the only other patrons in the room were in the far corner, their heads locked in quiet discussion. 'Apparently Rhys came to talk to her before I got back and they've gone somewhere—presumably the station? I don't know what's going on.'

Claire clutched her throat, her knowing eyes meeting his in wary shock. 'Oh no! I knew Rhys and James were questioning someone, but I didn't realise it was Ciara.'

Ginny leaned forward, and Sam repeated what he had told Claire in a low voice before she asked.

Like Chinese whispers, the information was quickly relayed to Kirk and Sophie before Ginny asked Sam where Briony was.

'In the kitchen helping Alex. There are four tables booked for dinner, plus Eleanor and us—and whoever comes in without a booking.'

Despite her busy day, Ginny gave Sam a firm nod. 'Right. I'll see what I can do to help them. Sophie, perhaps you could give Sam a hand and Claire, why don't you pop home and see if you can find out anything?'

'Mum!' Claire exclaimed in shocked tones. 'Are you suggesting I listen at the door?'

'Of course not,' Ginny hissed, throwing a glance toward the couple in the corner, who appeared to have not heard a word. 'I just thought you might check Ciara's alright. Maybe walk her back here ...'

Kirk pushed between them, speaking firmly. 'Neither of you girls are doing anything. Sam, would you mind pouring them both a drink please—and one for me? After that, I'll give you a hand here and Sophie and Claire can help in the kitchen and dining room. I'm sure that Rhys will be back with Ciara any moment and there will be no need for any of us to be worrying.'

Sam met his gaze with an appreciative swallow. It was good to have someone giving orders, especially as his thoughts were so scrambled, even pouring a beer into a glass seemed fraught with difficulty.

But deep within him, he knew it was only the beginning of what was to come.

INSISTING they stay until either Ciara returned or someone came to tell them why she hadn't, Ginny had made a pot of tea after Eleanor retired to bed and the last customer had left. Right on closing time, as Kirk helped Briony bring the pavement board in and close the front doors, an unmarked police car pulled up outside with the Featherwood Falls police vehicle close behind.

Sam glanced through the bar window as Rhys and James approached Briony and Kirk. Another man stepped out of the unmarked vehicle, leaving a woman in the back with Ciara beside her.

At the sound of car doors slamming, Sam urged Ginny, Claire, Alex, and Sophie to follow him, and they filtered into the foyer one behind the other as James stepped through the front door.

'Sorry to bother you guys at this hour of the night,' James said, turning to indicate the man behind him. 'This is Sergeant Davidson from the Australian Federal Police and the woman in the car with Ciara is Senior Constable McDonald. We're investigating a number of matters concerning the woman you know as Ciara King. Her correct name has been established as Naomi Kelly and we believe she is in possession of a number of items which will help us with our investigations. We have a search warrant for her room and personal property.'

He turned to face Sam. 'Can I speak to you for a moment in private?'

'Sure.' Sam led him across the foyer and into the tiny lounge, closing the door behind them.

'Interpol has advised Ciara's parents have reported her as a missing person,' he began. 'They were under the belief she is here in Australia. However, a check of records indicates she has never left the UK. This triggers a whole new range of questions we need to ask Naomi. Apparently, Ciara's parents received a message from her asking for ten thousand Australian dollars in April and she confirmed receipt by text of it a few days later. However, since then, they have not received any further communication and haven't been able to contact her. Are you able to tell us anything about this?'

'Good grief!' He drew a deep breath. 'There was a four-day period around that time when she left me in a youth hostel on the outskirts of Melbourne with the excuse she had business to attend to. Said she'd be back in a couple of days. When she didn't return and I couldn't contact her, I thought she'd ditched me but decided I'd give her another day or two. Then, just as I was leaving after giving up hope of seeing her again, she turned up as though nothing had happened and wouldn't tell me where she'd been. She insisted we leave Melbourne.'

'I see. Where did you go next?'

'We drove up the coast, spent a few days in the Coffs Harbour area. I thought we'd get work there and hang around, but she wanted to move on and go inland after I saw her talking to a couple on the beach. I asked her who they were but she said she didn't know them —they had confused her with someone else. Anyway we spent a while in the Dorrigo area but it poured with rain, so we ended up coming farther north and found work and accommodation here in Featherwood Falls.' He paused, rubbing his chin. 'What happens now?'

'I believe you share the room with Ciara so I'm sorry, we'll need to check your belongings too.'

'No problem,' Sam said.

He led James back to the foyer where the others were waiting.

'You can bring her in now,' James said to the officer.

Sergeant Davidson turned back to the car with James, who opened the door. Ciara stepped out with Senior Constable McDonald in front of her.

'Were you aware of this, Sam?' Kirk asked.

Sam shrugged. 'She's always been Ciara King to me.'

As Ciara passed Sam with barely a metre between them, he fell in behind her and asked softly, 'Are you alright?'

She turned and sneered at him. 'Don't you dare speak to me.'

While they disappeared down the hallway with Sam following, Rhys ushered Kirk, Claire, Alex, Sophie and Ginny into the dining room.

'WHAT'S HAPPENING?' Briony asked, her voice quavering. It had been a long, stressful evening and although physically exhausted, adrenaline pulsed through her veins as the puzzle of the baby's skeleton and the police questioning a young Irish woman who was working in her hotel stewed in her brain. Were they somehow connected? Considering Ciara was from Ireland, she would have been the last person Briony expected to give a DNA sample.

While Rhys indicated they all sit down, fear and incredulity rendered Briony immobile. 'What's going on? Why are the police here with Ciara?'

'Sit down.' Rhys's instruction sounded more like a command.

Alex pulled Briony onto the chair next to him and leaned forward, his elbows on the table as Rhys took the opposite seat.

'I'm not able to give you the full details of what is under investigation, but James contacted me earlier today,' Rhys began. 'He had received a call from Interpol. It appears Ciara King is somewhere in Britain—or at least has not left the country by normal means. That is, using her passport. And her parents have reported her as missing.'

Briony shook her head. 'But she's here? Working for us. Living with Sam.'

'We believe—and she has admitted, she is not Ciara King from Ireland.'

'Who the hell is she then?' Kirk exploded in disbelief. 'And what's happened to the real Ciara King?'

'Her name is Naomi Kelly, and she is Australian. The Irish accent is a cover.'

For a few moments, the only sound in the room was the ticking of a clock fixed on the wall above the kitchen door. Then everyone spoke at once.

'Oh, poor Sam.' Ginny said, unable to keep the shock from her voice.

'Bloody hell,' Kirk added.

'Gosh, how hard must it have been for Ciara to fake an Irish accent all this time,' Briony muttered.

'But why?' Ginny shook her head.

Rhys held up his hand to silence everyone. 'The search will take at least half an hour. What about we have a cup of tea while we wait—or something stronger if you'd prefer.'

Briony rose automatically to her feet, her mother following her into the kitchen.

At ten-thirty, James entered the room. 'I apologise for the shock this has given you. We have a number of items we wish to speak to Ciara about, so we'll leave you now. Thanks for your patience and cooperation.'

Sam appeared and stood beside the doorway, his face pale and solemn.

'What's happening with Ciara?' Briony asked.

'She'll be accompanying us to the Warwick station,' James said.

Rhys looked at Alex with an apologetic grimace. 'I don't suppose you could rustle up a takeaway meal for all of us? We haven't eaten yet. Of course, we'll pay for it.'

'Sure.' After jumping up as if relieved to escape the unfolding nightmare, Alex hurried into the kitchen.

Those remaining around the table shared wide-eyed glances before fixing their stares on Sam.

'Did you know Ciara wasn't who she said she was, Sam?' Ginny murmured quietly.

Seemingly unable to speak, Sam shook his head, his tall frame slumping into a chair as he reached for the glass of whisky Kirk offered him.

27

It was almost midnight before Sam's phone rang.

'Rhys?'

He nodded at the others before tapping the speaker icon and placing the phone on the table in front of him. After Rhys had departed with a pile of hot meals stowed in a brown-paper carry bag, the group had remained in the dining room, assuring Sam that despite their weariness, no one would go to bed until more was known.

'Yeah. I'm sorry it's taken so long to get back to you guys.' Pausing for a second, Rhys then said, 'I assume everyone is still there?'

'We are, Rhys—and the phone is on speaker so we can all hear what you have to say,' Ginny said.

'Great. At this point, all I can share is that we have

established Ciara—at least the woman who called herself Ciara—is actually Naomi Kelly. Unfortunately, she is not cooperating with us at the moment, but James and the Federal Police have taken her to Warwick overnight. There are a lot of unanswered questions that need investigating, including a quantity of cocaine and associated utensils found in her toiletry bag. However, some of the required checks will have to wait until office hours on Monday. Sam, did she use your laptop?'

'No, never—at least to my knowledge. It's locked and I've never shared the password with her. She didn't ask. Books were mostly her entertainment.' He rubbed a thumb and finger over his chin. 'So no, I'm sure she's never used it.'

'Thank you.'

'Will she be coming back here tomorrow?' Sam asked.

'She will not be eligible for a bail undertaking and will have to face court on Monday. She'll remain in custody until her appearance before the magistrate. No doubt she will apply for bail, and it is up to the magistrate whether she receives it or is deemed too much of a flight risk. I'll be in touch again after her court date.'

They finished the call and Claire stood, slipping her arms into her jacket sleeves. 'Good. I guess this is the downside of living at the station—getting involved whether you want to or not.'

Kirk put an arm over her shoulders. 'I'll walk you home.'

Ginny gave both Briony and Alex a quick hug. 'We'll pop back in the morning and give you a hand before our farm-stay guests arrive.' She shook her head. 'What a week.'

'I reckon.' Alex turned to Sam, who was still sitting with his chin resting on his hands and feeling dazed. 'Come on, mate. You look like you need a good night's sleep.' Alex slipped his arm through Sam's, encouraging him to stand up while Briony rested a hand on his shoulder.

'Are you alright, Sam? I know this is a shock for us all, but I can only imagine how you're feeling.'

Sam's troubled face cleared as he met hers and he straightened his shoulders. 'I've known I made a huge mistake for weeks now. She was so convincing. So caring and vivacious. But since we left Melbourne, she's changed. I know you guys haven't really seen it, but with me, she's become moody and ... kind of evasive. She doesn't look into my eyes anymore.'

Briony squeezed his shoulder.

'I thought I'd done something wrong to begin with —something to upset her, although I have no idea what.' He met Briony's concerned stare. 'Have you noticed she won't come anywhere with me? Since that weekend we had off and went camping at Girraween, whenever we've had time off together, she hasn't wanted to do anything except hole up in our room and read or watch movies.'

Briony started. 'I've just realised who she reminds me of. It's been in my mind for a while, but I didn't know why. Alex, remember that chef we worked with in Sydney for three weeks? He was arrested and charged with drug possession, and it was then we realised why he was either super nice or really nasty. The way Ciara's been behaving is similar and none of us even considered she might be using drugs.'

'I wonder if keeping whatever secrets she's been keeping has been eating away at her, creating a need for some sort of escape.' Alex spoke slowly, as though sharing his thoughts out loud.

Sam shrugged. 'Maybe. I know if I was pretending to be someone I'm not, I couldn't last more than a few minutes.'

A tiny chuckle escaped from Briony. 'Me too. And I think, given the events of today, that's a good thing.'

After saying goodnight and retreating to their rooms, Sam lay propped up on pillows, staring through the window into the backyard. Little moved in the darkened landscape except for the wind, howling through the clump of eucalyptus trees on the opposite side of the creek. Bit by tiny bit, the pent-up guilt and frustration that had gripped him for weeks seeped away, leaving a still-confused but resigned man. It hadn't been his fault. The unease that had grown in

Ciara's company was his subconscious telling him he should have listened to himself and, from the day he discovered the money and passports, should have done something.

He rolled onto his side and tucked his legs under the doona as the chilly night air seeped into him. Convincing himself the delay in sharing his findings with Rhys had done no harm—at least to anyone in Featherwood Falls—he closed his eyes and fell into a broken, troubled sleep.

IT WAS a weary team of workers who meandered their way around the hotel the following morning. Routine chores were done, food cooked, and the bathrooms and floors cleaned in silence. The first day of school holidays had arrived and with it, the first day of Eleanor's extended stay.

'Good morning.' The straight, well-mannered woman sailed into the dining room on the dot of eight, her hair knotted at the base of her neck, her face creased as though consumed with concern. Shuffling into the same chair at the same table she had done all week, she faced Briony squarely, who paused from wiping tables and straightening chairs to acknowledge her guest.

'Hello, Eleanor.'

'You look tired this morning, Briony. I noticed lights were still on when I got up to go to the bathroom in the night. Is everything alright?'

Briony shot her a tight smile. 'Sort of. It seems our Irish bar attendant isn't who we thought she was—in fact, she's not even Irish.' She slumped into the chair opposite the older woman. 'I guess we're all still in shock this morning.'

Eleanor fixed a startled expression on Briony, her eyes wide and enquiring. 'What's happened? Where is she?'

Briony hesitated before she spoke, reluctant to share what Rhys had told them with anyone outside the family—and yet wanting to say it aloud as though doing so would help her process the event. With a shrug of acceptance, she decided the story would be all around the town in no time, regardless of what she said, so better that it was the truth. She began.

'Oh dear,' Eleanor said, resting a hand at the base of her throat as Briony finished. 'It seems Featherwood Falls not only harbors history and buried bodies, but those who want to hide their identity too.'

'Yes. Who would believe it?'

'Well. I do.' Eleanor's voice was matter-of-fact and firm. 'My week here has been very interesting.'

Briony raised her eyebrows, waiting for Eleanor to continue.

'It's been lovely seeing Zoe again and hearing how

happy she is—and getting to know Lola and Frank, and Ryan and Emma, of course. But I've also found it fascinating visiting the cemeteries around the area and speaking with both Ned and Timothy, the historian I met. He's given me a list of procedures I shall undertake to establish my heritage. Evidently, asking the questions in order results in quicker answers.'

'How is Ned?' Briony asked, hoping Eleanor didn't mind the change of subject. 'We thought he'd be popping in daily to check on us, but it has been the opposite. I think the only time I've seen him was in the store one afternoon soon after the police started taking DNA samples. We were all delighted we weren't a match, but he seemed very quiet and I think a bit disappointed he wasn't.'

'Yes. He was a little. However, we both had morning tea with Lola and Frank the other day and he showed me some old photographs of his parents and their staff standing outside the front of this hotel when he was a little boy. I was surprised to see so many people. Quite a busy place back then. I guess the rooms upstairs would have been full of new settlers moving here and the constant seasonal workers.'

'I hadn't really thought about that. Gosh, if those two rooms we've just renovated were the family and staff quarters, they must have been jam-packed. They're not very big.' To steer the conversation away from Ciara, Briony turned to look at the painting on the wall above them. Waving a hand at it, she added, 'That's my great-great-grandfather with the horse and carriage. He was one of the early station holders and I believe a considerable force in this town. Must have been involved with this hotel or I don't suppose that picture would be here.'

'Most likely. I've been researching Featherwood Falls' early beginnings—mining, sheep farming and, of course, the fruit and vegetable growing that has evolved over generations. Apparently, this was a stock route. I'm not sure whether sheep and cattle were headed to or from Brisbane, but I guess that would have kept the hotel busy too.'

She paused, a small frown appearing on her brow. 'I may have to go home, Briony. Would you mind if I did that and returned after a few days?' Eleanor's voice took an upward tone, as though something might bring hope and excitement.

'Is everything all right?'

'Yes. I've received a reply to an enquiry I made several weeks ago. It's one I didn't expect to have success with—but I'm hoping it's good news.' Her voice rose slightly as she spoke.

Before Briony had a chance to question Eleanor further, Sam's appearance in the dining room distracted them both.

'I'll get your breakfast, Eleanor,' Briony said.

'Thank you, dear. I would like to speak with your

lovely young police officer before I return to Brisbane, and I don't like to disturb him on the weekend. Is it too much trouble for me to depart on Monday—and then return on Thursday?'

'It's no problem at all. Your room will be ready for you.'

'Wonderful. Now, I'll have the same as every other morning please—a small bowl of fruit, a soft-boiled egg, and two slices of toast. Oh, and a pot of English breakfast tea with milk.'

'Of course.' Briony smiled as she hurried away and swept into the kitchen.

'Eleanor would like the same breakfast as usual please.' She lay an arm over Alex's shoulders as he sat at the table planning the next week's menus. 'She's leaving us on Monday and will be back on Thursday. Has something she needs to attend to in Brisbane.'

'Okay.' Alex placed his pen carefully on the paper and rose to his feet.

'I'll be back in a tick. I'd better make that change in the diary now, before I get distracted elsewhere.'

They shared a chuckle as Briony dashed off again.

She had made the changes and was about to return to the kitchen when the shelf of old diaries caught her eye.

I wonder if there're any clues about the baby's birth in one of these. Stopping, she reached for the first of the 1930s hotel volumes. It fell open mid-book, and she cast a glance down the page, her eyes widening at the neat, precise column of names listed against room numbers. Extra details were written beside some names in tiny letters. Squinting, Briony focused on one note.

Extra care required. Difficult disposition.

With a wry smile touching her lips, she reflected on the hundreds of bookings she had taken in her hospitality career and the stories she could share if she dared. As she replaced the book and left the office, she decided she would begin reading tonight. *You never know—these could be as interesting as a novel.*

28

*S*ophie peered through the bedroom window, frowning at the purple, storm-laden sky. She had hoped the glorious crisp weather with frosty nights and clear, sunny days would welcome the new guests to Featherwood Falls.

Flash and Rusty, the two ancient ponies that were no longer fit to carry a rider but put up with as much grooming and fuss as anyone would provide, were ensconced in a large yard behind the stables with a roof over their heads and a view toward the homestead. The other three horses—Akela, Splash, and Tango—had been brushed daily until their coats shone, then wrapped in warm rugs and hoods and released into an adjacent, grass-lined paddock where Sophie could catch them with a minute's notice and have them ready to be ridden before the prospective rider had fastened their helmet.

Besides providing farm-stay guests with horse rides, Ginny had purchased a dozen fertilised eggs to put under a clucky bantam hen who, although long past laying herself, remained the most dedicated and fussy mother any chick could have. Sophie had settled mum and eggs into a warm, wooden nesting box Kirk had made for the purpose and tucked it inside a secure, two metre square cage inside the hay shed. A solid roof covered half of the pen, strong enough for children to sit on while they clutched newborn chickens in their small, sweaty hands, while the other half of the cage was coated with a fine wire mesh—sturdy enough to tolerate excited visitors but with small enough gaps to prevent crows or Currawongs poking their beaks through and stealing the tiny chicks.

During the September holidays, Ginny had assured Sophie there would be young lambs to hand-rear, even if she had to steal a triplet from one of her older ewes for a few hours each day to allow visitors to bottle-feed. However, during mid-winter, having newborn animals on the farm was rare and avoided. Thankfully, those guests who ventured away from the coast to experience a snippet of a granite-belt winter seemed content with witnessing heavy frosts, skating around on two-centimetre-thick ice in their smooth-soled runners. Having to break the sheets of ice in the animal troughs each morning added to the winter excitement, while huddling in front of a huge fire in the evenings, rugged up in woollen hats, gloves, and padded jackets, brought a rosy glow to their faces.

For most people, beginning an ideal holiday did not involve having to deal with torrential, freezing-cold rain and winds that whistled through every crack and crevice in the rustic shearer's quarters.

Sophie pulled on layers of clothing and slipped her feet into a discarded pair of Briony's sheepskin slippers before joining Ginny and Kirk in the kitchen.

'Hi, Soph. Did you sleep?' Ginny pushed a mug of tea toward her.

'Eventually. It took me a while though.' She frowned, shaking her head. 'Remember when I first saw Ciara, I mentioned she looked like someone I'd met in Scotland?'

'Oh, you did. I had forgotten that.'

'I couldn't stop thinking about it after I went to bed—and I think the girl I met was Naomi. That is, the Ciara who's here that we now know is Naomi. That was why she was so evasive and snooty toward me. I think she recognised me too—and that would have been the last thing she expected.'

Kirk leaned forward, his elbows on the table. 'So, if

you met her in Scotland, she must have been over there at some point.'

Sophie nibbled her lip. 'All I know is she was at the same party as me—and now she's here in Featherwood Falls. It doesn't indicate she's done anything wrong—especially as we now know she IS Australian and therefore would presumably have travelled back here on her own passport with no suspicion or question. Anyway, I'm sure the Federal Police would know that as they would have checked the flight records.'

Drawing a noisy breath, Kirk huffed it out. 'Yeah, true. Cripes, I wouldn't want to be a copper. So many possibilities and yet, if the suspect won't talk, where do you start? Might be worth mentioning to Rhys though.'

Ginny slid into a chair, both hands wrapped around the mug resting on the table. 'I agree with Kirk, Sophie. It may have absolutely nothing to do with her impersonating someone else. But she has been found to be in possession of a stranger's property and, if nothing else, it puts a timeline on where she was and at what point. Do you remember exactly where and when that party was, Sophie?'

'Sure. It's in my phone calendar. It was supposed to be an engagement party for one of the girls I worked with. But she broke up with her fiancé-to-be the week before and was so distraught, we talked her into having the party anyway to celebrate her freedom. Not sure if it worked though because she left Inverness a couple of weeks later and, last I heard, was heading for London.'

'So, you don't know how she knew Naomi?'

'No.' She paused, narrowing her eyes. 'I didn't know her and neither did my friend. She was at the pub when we arrived and latched on to us. Peeved us both off a bit actually, but my friend didn't let it worry her. Everyone was out to enjoy the night.'

'Okay. Well … to my untrained ears, I still think it's worth letting Rhys know. He can pass the information on to James in case they need to question her further about it or want to know more about who she is and what the story is with this missing Ciara,' Kirk finished with a frown. 'That's going to take a bit of detective work, I reckon.'

'Okay. I'll get my phone and check the date. Then I'll give Rhys a call.'

'Good.' Ginny beamed as she picked up Sophie's empty mug. 'I'll whip up some scrambled eggs while you ring.'

'No. I've got a better idea,' Kirk said. 'Today's Sunday, so we'll let Rhys have his day off and I'll take Sophie into town tomorrow. She can talk to Rhys face-to-face to ensure the details are clear and documented. You never know where this is going to lead.'

FEELING a little like it was she who had done something illegal, Sophie shared all she could remember about the party in Inverness and her introduction to Naomi.

Rhys looked up from his scribblings and asked, 'Did you know Ciara King?'

'No. Until I arrived here, I had never heard that name—but when I met her ... Naomi, I mean, I knew there was something familiar about her. And now you've told us that the person we thought was Ciara is actually Naomi, I realised why.'

'Thank you, Sophie. I'll get this information off to James and he'll take it from there.'

'Any news yet of Ciara's court appearance this morning?' Kirk asked.

'Yes. The magistrate has refused bail, and she has been remanded in custody for a month while the Feds conduct further investigations into the missing real Ciara.'

'Crikey,' Kirk said. 'This is getting serious.'

About to leave the station, Sophie took a backward step as Kirk opened the door and Mrs Worth, Briony's hotel guest, walked inside.

'Oh, I am sorry! Am I interrupting?' Eleanor clasped her handbag in front of her as she and Sophie almost clashed.

'No. It's okay,' Sophie mumbled, feeling the heat rise up her neck. 'We're just leaving.'

'That's alright then.' They exchanged positions and as the door closed behind her, Sophie overheard the woman say, 'I've come to discuss the matter of the deceased child found under the hotel's floorboards.'

Spangled sunshine sprayed the paddocks with golden light as it burst through the clouds over Featherwood Station. The rain had lasted only minutes before blowing northwards, leaving the foliage on the mock orange hedge dewy and sparkling.

Sophie was in her element. While Claire had taken the mother of the two children for a trail ride on Tango, Sophie and the little girls' father, who had introduced himself as Nick, were brushing Rusty and Flash. With unlimited patience, the ponies stood immobile with closed eyes, enjoying every stroke of the brush, even though the bristles focused on a single spot on their bellies rather than being long, even sweeps. Oblivious to the high-pitched chatter the four and six-year-old exchanged, Rusty's head drooped lower until his wobbling bottom lip almost touched the ground.

Relieved to have something to take her mind off the Ciara case, Sophie entertained the two girls and their dad for over an hour. Trailing around the house paddock, they fed hens, poured passionate love on the newly hatched chicks—requiring Sophie's nervous supervision in case they hugged the little creatures too tightly—and made friends with the dogs as she released them one at a time from their pens to not overwhelm the girls.

The pace increased the following day as a second couple arrived to stay two nights, and so did a car containing four teenagers who had booked a week of riding lessons. Because of varying experience, Claire allocated each rider a half-hour of one-on-one instruction while Sophie supervised the others, grooming and rugging the horses not being used before discussing names of various pieces of saddlery, demonstrating hoof cleaning, and mixing up horse feeds for the evening.

By the end of the day, it was not only the patient horses who welcomed their meal and a sleep but also Sophie, who decided that assisting with critical surgery on animals was significantly less exhausting than coping with a bunch of excited and emotional teenagers.

As she snuggled into bed later that evening, she remembered her promise to Briony. Until they knew what was happening to Ciara, she would help at the hotel on busy nights. Despite her exhaustion, a leap of anticipation filled her, wiping away all thoughts of teenagers and riding lessons. While she didn't have the training to assist in the bar, she had spent many years waitressing and serving customers at her mother's café. And being in the hotel would give her the chance to see Sam again.

With that thought in her mind, and a smile on her face, she drifted into sleep.

29

With less than two weeks until their grand opening, Briony ticked off the items on her list: meat and vegetables ordered; a trip to Warwick to purchase groceries and decorations planned; and the musician confirmed. She tapped the end of the pen against her cheek as she considered what she had forgotten.

Almost leaping off her chair as the phone rang beside her, she snatched up the receiver, reminding herself that she needed to have the bell in the hall removed—or toned down, if possible. Ned had said it was installed to cater for his failing hearing, but she found it disruptive and unnecessarily loud.

'Hello. Featherwood Falls Hotel. This is Briony.'

'Hello, dear. It's Eleanor.'

Briony blinked. The woman had only left to return

to Brisbane the day before. 'Lovely to hear from you again so soon.' She paused for a second. 'Is everything alright?'

'Oh, yes. Well, at least I think it is. I need to return to Featherwood Falls as soon as possible. I've arranged to meet Timothy Cross in Tenterfield as he has historical information to share.'

Briony raised her eyebrows. It sounded like a lot of driving for someone of Eleanor's age—but she understood Eleanor's ancestry journey. 'When are you planning to arrive?'

'Tomorrow? It's a day sooner than we discussed, but if my room is booked out, I can leave it another day.'

'You don't need to do that. Your room is available and waiting for you, Eleanor,' Briony said.

'Very well. I'll see you tomorrow and will ring Lola and advise her of my plans.'

After finishing their call, Briony entered the booking into the computer, checked the dinner reservations for the upcoming weekend, and headed for the kitchen.

'I'm glad we've got Sophie coming to help. With Ciara out of the scene completely, I wonder how we would have coped?'

Alex looked up from where he was rolling pastry dough, inclining his head toward the door as Sam appeared. 'How much longer have we got you, Sam?'

Sam shrugged. 'I'm not sure. I'm in no real hurry to leave. We've put you both in an awkward position and I'm really sorry about that.'

Briony stepped forward. 'Oh, Sam. I know how hard this must be for you. You trusted Ciara and had … well, lived with her for months now.'

'I've been a fool, and I'm pretty embarrassed about the whole thing. I'm glad to see the back of her.'

Briony tried to smile away her shock. When they had first arrived in Featherwood Falls, the couple had seemed in love, eager to live and work together. She reflected on the past few weeks. Sam had expressed his enjoyment at working on the farm—and seemed to enjoy both the renovations and clearing and converting the messy backyard into what now resembled a park, with or without Kirk's help. But ever since their weekend away camping, she admitted the atmosphere hadn't been quite the same. Ciara had still entertained the patrons, drawing a grin or a joke from even the most bitter and grumpy of locals. Her occasional bursts of song in a clear, perfectly pitched voice —usually a well-known Irish ballad or a Slim Dusty classic that everyone could sing along to—had drawn attention to her to begin with. But now Briony thought about it, the singing had been short-lived, even if her attention to customers had not.

'I'm sorry your stint in Featherwood Falls hasn't lived up to what you'd hoped.'

Sam flicked a palm in a stop sign. 'No! Please don't think that. I have loved my time here—still do. But I made a mistake. I thought Ciara was the one for me. Time and events have shown I couldn't have been further from the truth.'

'We all make mistakes and totally understand why and how you became so smitten with her. We did too —until recently when something seemed to change her. It was as though she lost her mojo, and at times, her manners—not to mention the accent which we now know was fake. That in itself must have been hard to keep up. I wonder if other secrets she's keeping have become too much for her—including what looks like may be a drug habit?'

He shuddered visibly. 'Dunno—but I guess we'll find out eventually. If she does have a drug habit, she's done a good job of hiding it from me. Anyway, if you'll excuse me for half an hour, I'd like to finish the mowing.'

Again, Briony and Alex exchanged glances. 'Absolutely,' they said in unison as he left the room.

30

———

*B*riony welcomed Eleanor like an old friend —her greeting reciprocated with a wide smile.

'It's wonderful to be back. I'm not sure what it is, but this town—and especially this community—has made me feel very comfortable.'

'I know what you mean. It has a kind of familiarity and cosiness to it—possibly because nothing changes.' Briony paused for a moment. 'Actually, that's not quite right. This time, I've discovered the town is growing. A few more houses dotted around, a second teacher in the school now—and our once-sleepy police station seems to be heaving with work.'

Eleanor raised her eyebrows. 'Shall I go up?'

'Of course. Your room is ready and here is the key.'

Briony handed the woman an old-fashioned door key, a disc engraved with the number three tied with a pink ribbon threaded through the loop at the end of the strong steel stalk. 'I'll put the kettle on.'

'Lovely. Thank you, dear. I shall be in the dining room in fifteen minutes.'

Something in Eleanor's demeanour piqued Briony's interest. The woman appeared younger and more energetic than she had a week earlier. From what Lola had shared and Briony had gleaned herself from Eleanor, the woman's Brisbane life had been both lonely and sedentary since Zoe's mother's death and Zoe's move from the apartment across the hallway to Featherwood Falls.

Lost in a cycle of questions and empathy, Briony filled the kettle and began preparing Eleanor's favourite midday meal of soup and thick, freshly baked sourdough bread while Alex stirred something spicy on the stovetop and sang along to his favourite playlist. The music was just loud enough to soften the conversation but still enable either of them to hear Sam's voice chatting to a customer in the bar next door.

Briony carried the tray containing Eleanor's lunch into the dining room, biting back the urge to question her guest. Clamping her lips together, she smiled and reminded herself that all good—and interesting things–come to those who wait.

THE FOLLOWING DAY, dressed warmly in slacks, stout boots, and the familiar burgundy coat, Eleanor waved to Briony as she passed through the hotel lobby.

'I'm picking Lola up and we're having lunch with Timothy. See you this evening.'

'Lovely. Have a great day and take care on that ice in the car park.'

Briony grimaced. The still, bitterly cold night had left a carpet of frost in all but the sheltered spots and the morning sun had still not reached the south side of the hotel where guests were encouraged to leave their vehicles. *Another thing we'll have to do when we have the money*, Briony thought. Carports had become standard behind or beside most country hotels she and Alex had checked out while calculating the costs of purchasing the Featherwood Falls Hotel. Providing shelter to keep the sun and frost off visitors' cars was not essential, but she was sure it would add a bonus for customers.

She hurried into the kitchen to run through the list of jobs still to do before the weekend's big opening.

Thanks to Claire's and Zoe's pre-school holidays trip to the surrounding towns and villages, posters were now on a number of shop and business windows. Frank and Ryan had added Claire's leaflets to the mail run and now every household in the area knew about the "Rebirth of Featherwood Falls", including relatives and friends of the town's residents who apparently were coming back to revisit old memories and see the changes for themselves.

When she dwelt on the thought of potentially hundreds of people filling their little hotel, spilling out the back and drifting down the lawn toward the creek, every nerve in her body twanged with a mixture of hope and fear. What if they ran out of food? Worse still, what if they ran out of drinks? Briony clamped her lips firmly together and shook her head. *That won't happen*, she told herself briskly. For days, Alex and Ann had been preparing every dish or part there-of that was possible to freeze, allowing the morning of the event to make massive bowls of pizza dough and gigantic trays of roast vegetables to go with the variety of meats that would be slow-roasting from early morning until late that evening.

Gluten-free and vegetarian options had been planned, now possible thanks to a completely separate set of cooking utensils, oven, refrigerator, and preparation area in the old scullery next to the main kitchen. Briony was certain no item had been forgotten and no one left uninvited. A quiver of excitement ran through her. The opening was almost as fraught with as much stress and organisation as their wedding would be— when they eventually had time to plan it.

DARKNESS HAD FALLEN, the fires blazing with warmth as customers filled the dining room before Eleanor's return.

'I'm sorry I'm late for dinner, Briony,' she said, unwrapping the scarf from around her neck as she walked in.

'Don't apologise, Eleanor. You said you'd be back this evening and you are. Did you have a good day?' Briony set out cutlery, glassware, and a freshly folded napkin on the corner table Eleanor commandeered.

'Oh yes. More than good, actually.'

Briony raised her eyebrows. 'Sounds interesting.' She glanced around the room, reassuring herself her patrons were not waiting for her attention. 'Let me get you a drink, then you can tell me about it.'

Eleanor dipped her head, unfolding the napkin and laying it on her lap. Leaning forward, she whispered, 'Would you mind if we had our chat in the lounge later?'

Nodding, she sped off to get Eleanor's drink. Whatever Eleanor wanted to share must be important—and too sensitive to reveal within earshot of other customers. But why tell Briony? Lola was the one who had become Eleanor's friend, and Zoe was virtually her pseudo-granddaughter. Briony was simply the owner of the hotel Eleanor had stayed at while she spent time with Zoe and explored the area.

Briony's head buzzed with possibilities as she looked forward to hearing what the older woman had to share.

ALMOST TWO HOURS LATER, Briony followed Eleanor into the tiny lounge room at the front of the hotel.

'We've located a member of my family.' Eleanor's voice was barely a whisper.

Creases formed between Briony's eyes. Why was Eleanor being so secretive about it?

'That was the first item on the list Timothy gave me —I had to find the surname of at least one of my parents.'

Briony blinked hard. Wasn't it the same as her own maiden name? Unsure where this was heading, she encouraged her to continue. 'Go on.'

Eleanor sat back on the sofa, resting her hands in her lap. 'It's a long story, but as you know, I came here because after Zoe left Brisbane, I decided to research my ancestry. I suppose her departure made me realise how important blood ties can be and, while it's often better not to know, I'm in my twilight years and wanted information about my family before I die.'

Briony nodded again, remaining silent to allow Eleanor to continue uninterrupted.

'I never knew my actual parents. I was adopted at two after being left on the doorstep of a convent in Brisbane as a baby and being cared for by the nuns. Then a kind and caring couple took me home and treated me like the much-wanted child they couldn't have. They told me when I was fifteen that I had been adopted, but as I had no memory of those first two years, I had no interest in searching for my biological parents. I had a happy childhood, although with no siblings it was a lonely one at times.' She shrugged, a small smile creeping onto her lips. 'My father was a school principal and taught me to read very young. He ensured I was well-educated, and I followed in his footsteps, becoming a teacher. My books and my students kept me busy and provided the comfort I needed, and my parents showered me with love.' She paused again, clasping her hands together in her lap. 'I met my husband in the late sixties at a dance hall in Brisbane they called Cloudland. They bulldozed it decades ago and now the area is a housing estate. Anyway, my husband was in the army and was to fly to Vietnam with his platoon—so it was a short courtship, a hurried wedding, and then ... sadly he was killed only weeks after leaving Australia.'

With tears welling, Briony held a hand against her chest at Eleanor's tragic story, despite the older woman's emotionless statement. 'I'm so sorry, Eleanor. That's awful. What happened then?'

'My husband and I both lived with my parents in the schoolhouse until he left for Vietnam, and a week before I received the news he had been killed, my mother died of a heart attack.'

Briony almost choked as empathy overwhelmed her.

'My father was devastated,' Eleanor continued. 'I had to nurse him as he wouldn't eat and lost the ability to care for himself. He passed away months later—a blessing.'

Briony reached over and lay a hand on Eleanor's. 'Does Lola know this?'

'Yes, she does. We've become friends, and I shared what I'd discovered with her earlier in the week. The government adoption records had answered my inquiries and provided more facts, including the name of someone who may be able to assist me, so I needed to return to Brisbane. That person was an elderly nun from the convent where I was left. She introduced herself as Sister Monica. She is of a similar age to me, so I was long gone before she joined the sisters. But she shared helpful memories of the childcare they provided in those days—and also confirmed how they worked with the government to find homes for abandoned children.'

'What else did she tell you?'

'Apparently, in the 1970s, she and another nun were tasked with clearing out cupboards full of records. They read a number of them as they boxed them up for storage. When the convent closed, Sister Monica moved into a house with three others and the records were archived. Fortunately, by then the authorities recognised the importance the documents had, and in my enquiries, some of that information was passed on to me. Once Sister Monica knew my approximate birth date—we believe it to be the ninth of April 1939—she remembered that file. Because leaving a baby on the doorstep was not a common occurrence, my file was one everyone recalled. Evidently, they kept whatever items came with each baby or child but relinquished only a toy or perhaps a shawl that the adopting parents asked for. Remaining items were listed in case they were needed to assist with identification.' Eleanor's voice had risen with the wonder of it all.

'Together with the blanket I was wrapped in, a scrap of paper with the words "Baby Johnson" was tied to my leg with a length of homespun wool. I don't know why they didn't trace my parents through that note, but they didn't and I feel it was an extraordinary fluke of good luck that the one nun who knew something about it was still alive and remembered the name!'

She shook her head slowly, as if the entire story was incomprehensible.

'The strange thing she recollected over all else was that scrap of wool. Apparently, it had the smell of lanolin on it so was likely to have been made by a sheep farmer or his wife. The lanolin had left grease on the cardboard file. That surname and the suggestion of sheep gave me something to begin my research with. That said, many records have been destroyed and there are a lot of families with the surname Johnson. I had thought the task quite hopeless before I met Timothy Cross. We have narrowed down timelines and areas with a high number of Johnsons living in them and began with this area because it was a well-established sheep-farming district around that time—and was within driving distance of the Brisbane convent.'

Briony felt pleasure for Eleanor but a little mystified about why she chose to share the information with her.

As though reading Briony's mind, Eleanor added, 'Please excuse me for rambling. I know you're probably wondering how I came to discover so much in a brief space of time—but we can thank the police for their assistance with that.'

'Oh?'

'I received some rather startling news this week.'

Briony leaned forward. 'More startling than discovering your family's past?'

'Yes.'

Briony waited a beat, her attention now fully focused on her companion. 'Can you tell me?'

'Soon after I arrived here—after hearing about the discovery in this hotel—I visited the police station and provided a DNA test. And that is why I'm being given so much help. Because so far, the only matching DNA to that poor little baby is mine.'

31

It seemed to Sophie the first week of school holidays flew by faster than any other time. With guests requiring farm tours, riding lessons, and walking guides to the old mining sites at the far corner of Featherwood Station, it was only when she joined Claire and Rhys at the hotel for their routine Friday night drinks and meal that Briony shared Eleanor's news.

While the revelation of a positive DNA match had boosted hopes of disclosing the true identity of the baby inside the hotel, the more mystifying issue of Ciara's sudden disappearance was on everyone's lips.

Sam and Briony were run off their feet behind the bar while Ann and now Zoe, who was helping them during the holidays, were in the frantically busy kitchen and dining room with Alex.

'Are you sure you don't need me, Briony?' Sophie fidgeted with her credit card before tapping it on the machine. 'I feel bad not helping.'

'This is good practice for the opening,' Briony declared as she passed the tray of drinks to Sophie. 'And no. Mum said you and Claire have had a hectic week. Treat this evening as a rest because I reckon I'll need all the help I can get tomorrow.'

'Okay. We'll be here in the morning as soon as we've fed the animals. Ginny warned the guests about our unavailability tomorrow, and no one seems to mind. They're going to have a look around the district and will join us here in the evening.'

The hotel buzzed with excited anticipation—not only about the following day's party but also about Ciara's absence.

'I'm sorry.' Briony's voice was firm and louder than usual in order to be heard over the chatter. 'We don't know any more about Ciara's situation than you at this stage. We've been hoping she would return to tell us, but the police have other ideas—obviously for good reason.'

Regardless of Briony's response, like the proverbial Chinese whispers, the gossip among the patrons continued.

THE FOLLOWING day dawned crisp and clear—the blue sky touched only by a few fluffy white clouds. Frost sparkled on the lawn and icicles hung from a dripping tap beside the newly restored outside washhouse where Sam was mopping the floor.

Their big day had arrived—the restoration of the tired hotel, complete with everything it promised was to be celebrated.

'Sam!' Briony called. 'Breakfast.'

With a final slosh of the mop, Sam squeezed it out, threw the dirty water over the lemon tree, and stood back to admire the array of fairy lights decorating the veranda.

'Everything looks beautiful.' Briony smiled at him. 'Thanks so much, Sam. I know these past couple of weeks have been hell, but we couldn't have done it without you.'

'I've enjoyed it.' His simple words surprised him. Gone was the aching head and sleep deprivation, his body responding like a robot and his emotions at their lowest ebb. Guilt, regret, and dread that at any minute Ciara would march through the door and blame him for everything had melted away as the days passed. There had been no further word from either the police or Ciara, and Sam had gradually returned to normal. It was the relief, he told himself. Relief from holding secrets, relief from tiptoeing around Ciara as her moods swung and her interest in him wavered, and relief that Briony and Alex were such caring and friendly employers. Not only employers. They were friends.

'I'd like to give Alex a hand in the kitchen this morning—at least until Ann and Zoe get here after lunch.' Briony had a list in her hand—a regular occurrence for her. 'Would you mind running the vacuum cleaner around the place, please?'

Sam grinned. 'Course I will. I'll stock the wood boxes and get the fires lit first, then I'll make sure I suck up the mess I make.'

It hadn't taken him long to acknowledge Briony's pressure points—and leaving evidence of wood and twigs on the hearth was one. Another was ensuring everything on her list was crossed off by the end of each day. He admired her organisation and wouldn't dare refer to her lists as being pedantic.

She patted him on the arm like a well-behaved dog as they walked inside, sharing a smile.

BY MIDAFTERNOON, the fragrance from the spit roasts drifted throughout the hotel and across the beer garden. Kirk arrived with Ginny and Sophie at nine, and they spent the entire day in cheerful harmony as they ticked off Briony's precious list of duties and transformed the plain century-old building into a pretty, welcoming party venue.

While Sam cleaned the lounge, bar, and dining room, Sophie turned the pile of flowers and greenery stripped from Ginny's garden into neat little posies and placed them on tables and sideboards. Balloons hung from the ceiling in colourful bunches, while the glassware and cutlery sparkled in readiness.

Sauces occupied every square centimetre of fridge space, accompanied by bowls of salads, jugs of caramel and berry coulis for the cheesecakes, whipped cream, and a massive tub of fruit salad.

While each of the helpers took turns to nip through the shower and change into their casual but smart "going out" attire topped with one of the new blue and white-striped aprons, Alex put the finishing touches to the humongous cake that would be shared at eight o'clock that evening.

The first arrivals trickled in soon after four-thirty, followed by a flood of couples, families, and more senior patrons on walking sticks or in wheelchairs. Glasses clinked as the musician set up in the corner of the bar, and as extra lights were turned on while darkness blanketed the town outside, the celebrations began.

NED TOOK pride of place beside the door, shaking hands as they entered and telling everyone how he knew it had been the right decision to sell the hotel to Briony and Alex. Briony's lips twitched as she passed him chatting to a couple he introduced as Rodney and Cherry—and overheard his high praise for the improvements Briony and Alex had made. It was not something she had expected, as she had worried he might feel jealous. She understood the difficulty many people had in accepting change—after all, there had been times in her own life when that had been the case. But for Ned, Briony acknowledged it must have been a massive obstacle for him to climb over.

Eleanor drifted around the dining room with Lola beside her, introducing themselves to every fresh face and catching up with those she had already met. In the far corner of the bar room, the musicians played request after request while couples danced on the polished floorboards and sang along at the top of their voices. Outside in the beer garden, families sat around the fire pit while children shrieked and ran up and down the gentle slope under the beam of numerous floodlights. By eight o'clock the main course had all but vanished, and Alex and Sam carried the enormous cake into the centre of the dining room. Everyone gathered around and, with no other appropriate song he could think of, Alex led the singing of "Happy birthday to the Featherwood Falls Hotel" in his broad Scottish accent.

As the hours flew, balloons popped and voices grew louder. Surprised at the number of patrons who sought her and Alex out to congratulate them, Briony's heart swelled with pride. The earlier, overwhelming feeling she'd had that their opening event would eclipse anything Featherwood Falls had seen in a long time had come to fruition.

AND THEN THE special event they had planned for weeks was over. They farewelled the last of the guests, locked the front doors, and flopped into the dining room chairs with those who had helped them create the special evening. Eleanor lowered herself onto a stool, her cheeks flushed.

'Fabulous evening,' Ginny croaked, her voice rasping with overuse and a wide beam on her face. 'I'm certain the takings will have outstripped your expectations. Perhaps now you'll be able to install the solar panels you want.'

Briony blew out a whooshing breath of relief. 'I hope so.' She turned to Eleanor. 'It was lovely finally meeting your friend Timothy.'

'Was he the gentleman with the white beard?'

Sophie asked. 'I'm sorry I didn't have time to stop and talk to you both.'

'Quite understandable, dear. Yes, that was Timothy Cross—an appropriate name for a retired vicar, I think.'

They all laughed before she continued.

'He has provided me with an enormous amount of information, which I'm sifting through—and now Ned is feeling less tired since moving, he is also keen to revisit the suitcase of photographs from the hotel and see if anything interesting pops up.'

'I'm making a pot of tea,' Sophie announced. 'Anyone else want one?'

A volley of yes's followed as Sam rose to his feet. 'I'll give you a hand.'

Briony watched them leave the room before meeting Alex's gaze. She shot him a grin, and he winked back. While Sam and Sophie had beavered away all evening serving drinks and providing customers with hot chocolate and coffee from the new machine, their relaxed camaraderie had not gone unnoticed. Despite Ciara's popularity over the past few weeks, it seemed Sophie's open and friendly attitude was even more welcome.

Kirk cleared his throat, attracting attention from his companions. 'I could be wrong, but I reckon Sam has recovered from his disastrous relationship with Ciara.'

A general titter of agreement circled as Alex added, 'And I couldn't wish a better friend for Sophie.'

32

The following morning, Kirk, Ginny, and Sophie returned to help Alex, Briony and Sam clean up and return the hotel and grounds to normal.

Having farewelled their weekend house guests who, as previous residents of the area, had driven from western Queensland and northern New South Wales to attend the official opening, Briony was mopping the floors when Eleanor poked her head around the door.

'I'm going out for the day but shall be back for dinner.'

'No problems, Eleanor. Enjoy your day.' Briony paused. 'Going somewhere exciting?'

'I believe it could be. Frank and Lola are collecting Ned and me, then we're meeting Timothy in Tenterfield,' she finished with an eager smile.

Briony's eyes widened. 'Wonderful.'

An hour later, with the hotel restored to its pre-event tidiness, Claire and Rhys arrived with perfect timing and headed straight to the coffee machine where they made everyone a hot drink.

The family gathered around the table with Sam as Rhys pulled out a folded piece of paper from his pocket. 'It's a shame Eleanor's not here. I've been reading the police diaries from the 1930s and I think I've found something that might interest her.'

Ginny leaned forward, her elbows on the table. 'Really? Can you share?'

'I suppose I can talk to Eleanor tomorrow about it. It may be nothing anyway, so I don't think she'll mind if I tell you guys.' He unfolded the paper and smoothed it with the side of his hand.

'I'm sure she won't. Go on,' Claire added.

'There's not a lot of interesting stuff—mainly comments about the potential war on the other side of the world and a few stock thefts. But there are three references during 1938 where the police challenged a drover for loitering around town. His excuse was that he was waiting to speak with his boss who was staying in the hotel, which I thought was a bit odd—I mean, why bother to note that? I would have thought there were more serious events to record.'

'Maybe his boss was someone important and the police omitted to write that down?' Kirk suggested.

'Is there any indication of who his boss was?' Briony asked.

'Oh yes. Jim Johnson or James Johnson. The names vary.'

Briony sat bolt upright. 'That's the surname Eleanor's been given from the nun she spoke to. It's the family name she searched for while she's been with us.'

'It's sounds as though you and Eleanor have had quite a chat,' Kirk said.

Briony chewed on a thumbnail. 'We have, and she mentioned she'd received help from the police. But it's Eleanor's story and I'm not sure if I should tell anyone.'

'But isn't Eleanor trying to establish a connection with the baby?' Kirk shook his head in confusion. 'I would have thought this information might be related to the mother she's looking for.' He met Briony's gaze. 'Why don't you tell us what you know? Perhaps we can put some of this puzzle together.'

'I guess so.' Briony drew a deep breath, tilting her head slightly. 'Eleanor told me she knew she was adopted, but, as with most people born in that era, knew nothing about her biological parents. She's been seeking evidence to suggest her surname at birth was Johnson. Now she believes she has it, along with confirmation she is a DNA match with the baby. So, the next step to tracking the connection is to find the name of the child's father, which is why she's accepted

Timothy's help. He seems to understand this business of searching for family history better than anyone else I've ever heard of.' She straightened, raising an eyebrow as she added, 'Not only is he an experienced and confident ancestry researcher, but his family has lived in the area for generations.'

Briony paused and glanced around at her companions. 'Perhaps I should call her and tell her about your discovery, Rhys. It's still weird though. I mean, why would someone bury a baby under the floorboards? If it was a legitimate birth, and this Jim Johnson is the father, wouldn't the child have been buried in the cemetery and have a name?'

'Maybe the child was illegitimate or because of its deformity, the parents didn't want anyone to know?' Ginny drew a deep breath. 'Things were very different back then. So much was hidden—and who knows, maybe Featherwood Falls was a judgemental environment and the mother feared ridicule and even ostracisation.'

'Or—the mother was staying here in this hotel and didn't want the community to know about the child.' Claire held up her palms in question. 'With the police mention of the drover's boss being Jim Johnson, it would be interesting to see if there was a Mrs Johnson staying here at the same time?'

Briony leapt to her feet. 'The hotel bookings! We've got all the books dating back to the 1930s in the office. I only started reading them a few nights ago and I haven't got far. I'll grab the ... did you say 1938?'

Rhys nodded.

'Be back in a tick.' Briony dashed into the hallway, her footsteps tapping lightly on the boards as she hurried to the office.

Within minutes, all heads were crowded around the book, attempting to match up the approximate dates with the police notes. During the first and second corresponding weeks, almost two months apart, every room in the hotel had been allocated.

'Maybe there was a function here,' Ginny said.

'Possibly.' Briony ran her finger down the column, announcing each name, while Claire jotted them in a spreadsheet format.

Flicking through the until she reached the third date matching the police files—one giving a six-month period since the previous—she stopped. Only two room reservations had been entered with a note scrawled across the top of each page "Bowens in Sydney. Bob and Laurel Mendel in charge".

Briony frowned as she read the details out loud. 'Bowen is Ned's surname, so it sounds as though his parents went to Sydney for a period and these Mendels cared for the hotel while they were away.'

'It does.' Ginny peered over Briony's shoulder at the page. 'The reservations were made in the name of Mrs Beryl Carlton ... and Jim Johnson.' She glanced at

Claire. 'Isn't Carlton one name Briony has read before?'

'Yep. It sure is.'

For a few seconds, all eight of them exchanged silent stares before Ginny spoke. 'I believe it's time to call Eleanor. Do you agree, Rhys? We wouldn't be overstepping police protocol, would we?'

'I doubt it, but I'll check with James. He'll want to know what we've found anyway.' He stood and crossed the hallway to the lounge.

They waited, fidgeting in silence as Rhys's deep tones murmured indistinctly across the hallway.

Eventually, Ginny rose. 'We need more coffee.'

She and Sophie disappeared into the kitchen before returning to the table, each carrying a tray of steaming mugs when Rhys returned.

'And?' Briony was the first to speak. 'What did he say?'

'He'll share the news with his team and gave us permission to contact Eleanor to pass on our discovery. The next question is the coincidence of Jim Johnson and Beryl Carlton both being guests here at the same time. Perhaps they were having an affair and are the parents of the dead baby?'

'I'm calling Eleanor now! I'm sure she and Timothy will find out more.' Briony strode from the room as the group exploded with a barrage of possibilities.

THE DAY DRAGGED as they waited for Eleanor to return. Although each continued with their duties, phones rang at regular intervals, all with the same question. 'Is she back yet?'

Eventually, at eight-thirty that evening, as Alex was packing away the remnants of the night's menu ingredients and both Briony and Sam were listlessly wandering around restocking shelves in the empty bar, a vehicle pulled into the kerb outside.

Doors slammed, and the sound of Lola's laugh reached them.

'They're here!' Briony called toward the kitchen as she hastily wiped her hands on a towel.

With Eleanor leading, Lola and Ned followed her into the lobby with Frank close behind.

While she removed her hat and scarf, Eleanor shared a beaming smile with them all. 'What a day!'

Briony nodded, silently urging her to divulge what she hoped would be positive news. 'Let's sit in the lounge while you tell us all you can.'

Alex appeared, and the seven of them filed through the doorway. Squished together on the tiny sofas with fat, satin-covered cushions behind them, all but Sam made themselves comfortable, leaving the remaining armchair for him as he stoked the cosy orange glow behind the fire screen until flames leapt and danced in the grate.

'Should I ring Rhys and Claire? So you don't have to repeat yourself?' Briony asked.

Eleanor shook her head. 'No. It's early days and we still have to liaise with the detective team to ensure we have the facts, given the time lapse.' She smoothed her skirt, crossing her ankles before she continued. 'However ...' She paused while everyone fixed their gaze on her as though willing her to unload a lifetime of secrets. 'We confirmed a couple by the name of Carlton lived on the northern outskirts of Tenterfield during the pre-war years. Charles Carlton was a retired air force commander who married in England, brought his wife, Beryl, who was a good few years younger than he, to Tenterfield. A newspaper article reported their welcome—he must have seemed important to Tenterfield society unless there was not much other news to share. Anyway, Charles Carlton was recalled to England because of the suggestion of war brewing in Europe, leaving his wife behind—presumably for safety.'

'What about Jim Johnson?' Briony asked. 'What was the connection between him and Featherwood Falls?'

'He was a grazier—a landholder of some note. Bought and sold sheep regularly—that much was clear in the newspaper records. He used a drover to move sheep between the New England and Darling Downs regions—and much of their wool was sent to the Ipswich Woollen Mills.'

'Eleanor ...' Briony interrupted, a confused frown on her face.

'Yes.'

'Do you think there's a connection between the piece of wool used to tie your name tag to you as a baby outside that convent—and Jim Johnson or one of his workers?'

Eleanor nodded silently. Everything and everyone in the room stilled—as though not daring to breathe.

'And you're thinking that this man—the sheep grazier—could be your father?' Briony continued, her heart pounding.

'Yes.' Eleanor took a deep breath. 'I'm positive of it.'

33

———

With more than two weeks still to pass before Ciara's court case and a surety from Rhys that her current charges would keep her in custody for a further period, Sam continued to worry. Cursing his earlier judgement, he reflected on the confession he'd made to Sophie the night of the party.

'I wish I had never met her.'

She had looked at him mutely with clear grey eyes for a long minute before she spoke. 'I understand how you feel. I've made mistakes too. But, if things had been different, and we hadn't made those mistakes, you wouldn't be here and neither would I.' Then she had smiled at him with such generous warmth that he'd felt a burst of optimism.

'True. I've got my sister to thank for that.'

'Your sister?'

'Yeah. She was always going on at me about my sheltered life. Living in a small country town didn't teach me much about the rest of the world, or the people in it. I guess I didn't care. I was happy staying home and working with Dad, whereas she was always flipping through magazines and raving about travelling and being a fashion model.'

'And is she?'

'A model? For a while. Now she lives in London and works in one of those fashion houses where famous people buy their made-to-fit clothes.'

Sophie had raised an eyebrow, their conversation cut short as Alex called her to help in the kitchen.

WITH ANOTHER WEEK of school holidays ahead, Featherwood Station's farm-stay cabins were booked out, and the hotel had reservations for the following weekend. The village swarmed with coastal visitors who had come to experience frosty, fire-warmed nights and taste the wine and fruits of the region. Thankful for the busy workload, Sam filled his days keeping the wood boxes stocked, weeding, watering, and mulching the trees and gardens, and spending longer than usual taking care of customers, local and otherwise, while the remaining threads of culpability faded.

'It's quite extraordinary that the very town that is

now home to Zoe could also be where my family roots began,' Eleanor announced at breakfast. Her fresh energy seemed to have brought hope and friendship from unexpected avenues. 'Timothy is driving up tomorrow and we plan to spend the day helping Ned sort through his photos.'

Sam smiled. His own grandparents were enthusiastic genealogists, so he'd had a taste of the extraordinary lengths people were prepared to go to in order to find not only their heritage, but to relive the lives of generations before them.

After the previous weekend's party and new historical discoveries, Eleanor had extended her stay in Featherwood Falls, declaring she would remain until she had exhausted every thread of information leading to her biological parentage—provided there was a room available in the hotel.

Together with Timothy's copy of the original property plan detailing the land settlement of the New England and Darling Downs areas, Eleanor's enthusiasm had risen to another level following the revelations of a possible connection between Jim Johnson and Beryl Carlton.

As Sam repetitively bent and straightened, emptying boxes of bottles and arranging them in the glass-fronted refrigerator, he let his mind drift from Eleanor to the real Ciara, still somewhere on the other side of the world. *Her parents must be desperate to find her*. His stomach clenched with empathy. The last James had advised was that they still did not know where she was or even if she was alive. Having been tricked into sending a huge amount of money to Australia, believing she was having the holiday of her life, had apparently crushed them beyond belief, and he was sure that even though their money had now been returned, it would have been of little consolation.

They must be devastated. He wanted to say how sorry he was. But he didn't know what to apologise for. Until he knew more about Naomi and how or why she came to have Ciara's identity documents, he felt useless.

Not only that, but the more time he spent with Sophie, the more he liked her. The desire to get away from Featherwood Falls had diminished and his head filled with confusion.

SCHOOL RESUMED, the hotel and village quietened, and a week of rain set in. While Claire completed several new design projects and her annual tax documents, Sophie wrapped herself in her oilskin coat and with gumboots on her feet, helped Ginny feed ute-loads of hay to the cattle and sheep.

With the Thursday quiz night approaching, Sophie spent the evenings in her room with the laptop propped in front of her, pouring over commonly asked questions and brushing up on her geography. This week she was determined the team comprising herself, Zoe, Sam, and Kirk would win—or at least come a close second. Ginny had been roped in to join Frank, Lola, and Ryan, as Emma's pregnancy was advancing and her exhaustion increasing. She had declared late nights were out for her—much better to stay at home with a good book—and Sophie had jumped at the chance to fill the vacant spot.

An email notification popped up, distracting Sophie. She clicked on it, her heart thumping as she read the details. Having reached the end, she read it again, then lay back against her pillows.

After clicking into Google maps, she zoomed in on central Queensland and, in particular, the town of Winton.

When she had applied for several regional positions the previous week, she had concentrated on the coastal areas, hoping to jag a job around the Whitsundays' or Cairns. The vacancy for a station hand on an outback property near Winton had flicked up amidst the hospitality positions on the coast. Something about the advertisement appealed, and she'd hit reply.

Now she had the offer to join the team on Cranwell Station, forty kilometres north-east of Winton. Her duties would vary but would predominantly include mustering, branding, medicating, and preparing cattle for sale, and working with the owners of the property in their Australian stock horse stud.

A shiver of excitement ran through her. The offer clearly stated the position would be for three months —until the couple's daughter recovered from a riding accident sustained weeks earlier. *That'll suit perfectly. After that, I'll move on and visit somewhere else.*

A vision of Sam's face flashed before her. Saying goodbye to him would be hard—especially as they got on so well and, unless she had imagined it, the spark that had ignited at their first meeting was morphing to a slow burn.

She lay there for long minutes, reading the email again. Then she closed the computer and wandered into the living room, where Ginny and Kirk were engrossed in a movie.

'Come and sit down. We're watching *The Equalizer* —for about the sixth time.' Ginny laughed and patted the couch beside her.

Sophie sat, waiting for the opportunity to voice her thoughts.

Half an hour later, Kirk pointed the remote at the television, silencing it as he rose to his feet. 'Hot chocolate, anyone?'

'Sure. Love some,' Sophie said.

'Count me in.' Ginny faced Sophie and lifted an eyebrow. 'You look as though something's on your mind. Want to share?'

Sophie licked her lips, uncertain how to begin. Ginny and Kirk had been so welcoming, so generous with their time—and their wages. She had learned new skills while being able to spend time with her brother's family-to-be. Not only that but catching up with Briony and Alex in the evenings, and on special occasions like their grand opening, had been priceless.

'I'm thinking of moving on. Seeing more of this lovely country and ...' She trailed off as Ginny wrapped her in a hug.

'Of course you should—and while you're welcome here anytime, the last thing we want is for you to feel you have to stay. This is your chance to get out into the world, explore Australia.'

The load lifted from Sophie's shoulders, and she straightened. 'I've been offered a position on a property near Winton.'

Kirk handed Sophie a steaming mug before plonking himself on an adjacent armchair. 'Perfect. I agree with Ginny. We appreciate all you do around here, but it's time for you to see more. Get a real feel for the country.'

'Will you be alright? I mean, spring isn't far away and I know you've got a lot of sheep to be shorn.'

'We've managed for years, Sophie. Don't think about it. Do whatever you want to now, while you've got the chance,' Ginny said.

'Thanks. It's only for three months, so I might be back for Christmas.'

'Great! This year, we'll have a proper family Christmas with Briony and Alex here again—and you are part of our family.' Ginny lay a hand on Sophie's and squeezed it. 'I think you'd better nip back to that computer and send them an acceptance email.'

34

It was following her team's jubilant win at the quiz night that Sophie told Sam about her new position.

'Congratulations!' While he voiced the word, his heart sank. 'When will you be leaving Featherwood Falls?'

'In another week. I've spoken to my new employers —their names are Debbie and Mark—and they said their property is soaked after heavy rain. Apparently, the homestead and buildings are three kilometres from the highway and it's a dirt road into the place. They suggested I catch a bus to Winton and they'll pick me up from there.'

Their eyes met as they stood in silence.

'I'll miss you,' Sam whispered.

'And I'll miss you, too. It's been great working

together—even though the last few weeks have been ... well, stressful for you, I suppose.'

'I've been wanting to move on—get away from the Ciara business—but I didn't want to leave before the opening and thought I should hang around until we know Ciara's verdict.' He heaved a sigh. 'I feel responsible for the trouble we've caused Alex and Briony.'

'It wasn't your fault though.' Sophie frowned and reached for his hand. 'We all know that—and we knew you were only going to stay a short while. Like me, our primary aim is to see Australia, and both Alex and Briony understand we're on a limited time frame to do that.'

'Yeah. Not sure where I want to go now though—or what I want to do.'

'I'll text you the name of the employment platform I went through. They seem to specialise in short-term positions for travellers. You never know. Something might pop up that interests you—just like this position did for me.' She shrugged. 'I'm not an expert with horses and this job consists of a lot of horse work.'

Creases formed between Sam's eyes. 'I hope you'll be safe?'

'Of course I will be. I'm not afraid—and I've learned so much since being on Featherwood Station.' She grinned. 'It'll be fun—and if it's not, it'll be an experience I'll tell my children about in years to come.'

'Are you two joining us for a celebratory drink?' Kirk's voice jolted Sam's attention away from Sophie.

'Yeah. Sorry, I'll get them.' Sam strode toward the bar, fixing his gaze on Briony's knowing smile.

'She's told you she's moving north, hasn't she?'

'Yeah.' In an attempt to avoid the conversation he wasn't ready for, he reached for a glass and grabbed the beer tap, turning away from Briony as he drew the frothy liquid. A muscle twitched in his neck as his phone pinged in his pocket.

Ignoring it while he filled drink orders, his fingers itched to check if the message was from Sophie with the details of the employment company.

'You know you can leave at any time.'

Sam jumped at Briony's murmured comment. He had been so focused on Sophie as she chatted with Lola and Ryan, he hadn't realised Briony was standing right next to him.

'I ...' He began. His chest tightened as though someone was sitting on him. 'I don't want to let you down, Briony.'

'Pfft. Don't be silly, Sam. Alex and I knew you were only stopping here for a short time—even though it's turned out to be a bit more dramatic than either of us expected.' She chuckled. 'You've helped us achieve a lot and have become more than an employee. You're now a personal and welcome friend.' She batted a hand toward him. 'If it's time for you to move on and see more of this country, then do it and stop feeling guilty,' she finished with a smile as she stepped forward and hugged him. 'Now take that tray of drinks to table seven and we'll talk more about this in the morning. Okay?'

He shot her a grin and nodded. 'Yes, Mum.'

SAM WAS LIGHTING the dining room fire the following morning when Rhys and James entered the lobby. The urgent tap of Briony's footsteps prevented Sam from intervening, and he paused, his ears straining to hear what was being said.

'Eleanor's on her way. Would you like to go into the lounge?'

Voices murmured and a door closed, heightening Sam's attention. A few moments later, the door opened again, and Alex's broad accent penetrated the silent air. 'This way, Eleanor.'

Alex's head popped around the doorframe. 'James wants to speak with Eleanor and has asked Briony and I to join them. Will you be right with everything here?'

'Sure,' Sam said as Alex disappeared again, closing the door tightly behind him.

Whatever is going on, it must be serious.

While he waited for the conversation to conclude, Sam tidied the glass cabinet and wiped surfaces. The floors needed vacuuming, but he didn't dare make a noise in case he missed reservation calls. As he wandered around half-heartedly, he reflected on his actions the previous evening. Although it had been late when he opened his laptop, he had searched for the company Sophie had messaged him and trawled through vacancies in the Winton, Longreach, and Hughenden areas. It appeared the hospitality industry was the major employer, and he completed an application for two hotels in Winton and a Tourist Park in Longreach before scrolling through opportunities at Cobalt Gorge and Mareeba.

Checking his phone at ten-minute intervals in case one of them had responded, he moved into the dining room and set tables before sitting down and folding a pile of serviettes into the shape of Bishops hats—exactly as Briony had taught him.

Forty-five minutes later, he shot to his feet as a door opened and voices echoed down the hallway.

Alex, Briony, and Eleanor appeared in the dining room seconds after the front door banged.

With one glance at them, the hairs lifted from the back of his neck. 'Everything alright?' he asked.

Briony shook her head. 'We need strong coffee and something to eat, Sam. Let's get that organised and we'll let Eleanor share her latest news.'

Fifteen minutes later, after Eleanor had sipped two cups of tea and chewed her way through a piece of toast, she lay her hands in her lap and faced Sam. 'I'm sure everyone in Featherwood Falls will know soon, but I believe it will help me come to terms with what the police have discovered by speaking it out loud—and I guess there's no other person who needs to know more than you.' Her face softened, her faded eyes misting over.

Puzzled, Sam leaned toward her and shared an encouraging smile. 'Please ... go ahead.'

'As you know, my friend Timothy has been assisting me on my journey to discover exactly who I am and where I came from.' She coughed and dabbed her mouth with a lace-edged handkerchief. 'It seems my biological parents were Beryl Carlton and Jim Johnson—at least as much as can be established with the information we have. Of course, we had suspected that might be the case a week or two ago, but what the police have found is that both Jim Johnson and Beryl Carlton died soon after the last time they stayed in this hotel.'

Sam straightened in shock, his interest growing.

'Jim Johnson died in a car accident after leaving Featherwood Falls to return to New South Wales—and Beryl Carlton took ill that same day. It seems the hotel managers at the time arranged for her to be transported to Brisbane, where she died of blood poisoning. The missing link is who took her to Brisbane. We only know she was outside the Royal Brisbane Hospital with only a purse containing a comb, handkerchief, and ten pounds. The bag she'd left here was returned to her home in Tenterfield, and it was only when Ned's parents returned and her room was cleaned that a card was found addressed to her and her husband, leading to the confirmation of her identity.'

While Eleanor cleared her throat and sipped more tea, Sam's frown deepened.

'If Beryl is your mother, then where were you when she died?'

'The police are certain that whoever took her to the hospital must have known she'd had a baby and also realised how sick she was. They believe that either before or after she was deposited at the hospital, I was anonymously delivered to the convent.'

'Wow. That's a lot of heartbreak to take on. So, the police believe, thanks to the hotel records, that Beryl and Jim WERE in a relationship—that Beryl became pregnant with him and the baby was born here?' Although empathy for the woman filled Sam, he struggled to find the connection between Eleanor's ancestry journey and what he had to do with it.

As though having read his mind, Eleanor continued, 'We can't be sure, but Timothy has been speaking with the family who now own the Carlton property. It seems there were rumours at the time of the woman who'd lived in their house becoming pregnant and trying to hide it. She disappeared in 1939 and never returned. There are those who said her demise was punishment for cheating on her husband.' Eleanor clasped her hands together. 'Of course, we have no proof but believe if that was true, and Beryl was pregnant by Jim Johnson, then that may well have been the reason the baby was born, died, and was buried here. It's quite possible that no one ever knew about that baby—although you would think there would have been an awful smell.'

'Not necessarily,' Rhys said. 'If the box had been airtight at the time and no one was sleeping in that room for a while, any unusual smell that permeated would probably have been blamed on the outside toilets or a blocked drain.'

'How awful for the parents,' Briony said.

Eleanor nodded. 'Again, we don't know what their situation was. If Jim and Beryl were both considered upstanding members of society, perhaps Jim didn't know Beryl was pregnant until that last meeting they had here, six months after the previous liaison. He may not have wanted to reveal his connection with a child.'

'I'd say that would have given him a surprise,' Sam said.

'Yes, Sam.' Eleanor lifted her chin. 'However, the biggest shock of all is that I was a twin—and my twin sister was that skeleton you discovered under the floorboards in this hotel.'

Briony raised her palms to her face. 'You and your sister were born right under this roof.'

Eleanor nodded, shrinking into her chair as though deflated after the revelation of it all.

'I still don't get why the baby couldn't have been buried in the cemetery,' Alex said brushing a hand over his chin.

'I'm sure none of us can,' Rhys said. 'And we'll probably never know. But at this stage, the police are suspecting Jim Johnson probably paid someone to arrange the burial—unless he refused to acknowledge the twins were his and washed his hands of it all. That could explain his accident going home. But whatever the outcome, the Mendels would have had to have known.'

'Or ...' Briony narrowed her eyes. 'Perhaps everything happened before the baby could be buried— Jim's accident, I mean, and Beryl getting sick and having to be taken to Brisbane with the surviving baby, then dying. So, the Mendels buried the baby here and kept the money.'

'Possibly,' Rhys said. 'There's no mention in any documents about who or what type of characters these people were. Perhaps they thought Ned's parents would somehow blame them for allowing a pregnant woman to give birth here instead of arranging for her to go to hospital. As I said, we will probably never know. But what we do know is that Eleanor has found her parents and is now the only living relative we can find of the deceased baby—her twin sister.'

'So as soon as the baby's remains are available, I will arrange to have her buried in the Featherwood Falls cemetery.' Eleanor rose, her face pale, and rested a hand on the back of the chair to steady herself. 'Now, if you don't mind, I need to lie down.'

Briony jumped to her feet. 'I'll walk you to your room, Eleanor.'

Without a word, the tall, stoic lady allowed Briony to lock elbows with her and they glided gracefully out of the room.

35

*W*hile surprise reverberated around the village, Briony focused on finding part-time staff and ensuring Eleanor recovered from her shock.

One of the Winton hotels had accepted Sam, and he was to begin his new role as bar attendant as soon as possible. While this news was exciting for both Sam and Sophie, Briony couldn't help but experience a massive sense of loss. It was as though the restoration of the hotel had brought them all together in a way she hadn't considered possible. With Ciara gone and now Sam and Sophie about to join forces and head north, a hole had opened up in the village's heart—one that would take time to fill.

Eleanor and Lola discussed the advantages and disadvantages of living in the country with Briony and

Alex, touching on the possibility of Eleanor selling her Brisbane apartment and moving to Featherwood Falls.

'It depends on what you'll be leaving in Brisbane and what medical services you'll need if you live here,' Briony said.

'Perhaps I'll put my name down for one of those little cottages where Ned is,' Eleanor announced. 'And if I can't drive and I need a doctor, I'll pay for a taxi or stay here and die in my bed.'

'You'll do nothing of the sort,' Lola argued. 'While the distance to a hospital is significant and getting to appointments could be tricky, in the future if you're unwell or can't drive, we're here. And as long as we're able to, we'll pitch in and ensure everyone gets where they need to go.'

In the end, Briony ignored the heated discussions and was relieved when Eleanor decided to return home the following week and think about her future plans—after she had first waved goodbye to Sam and Sophie.

PURPLE AND PINK streaks decorated the winter sky as Kirk lugged Sophie's suitcase down the steps. 'I reckon you're taking a lot more away with you than you arrived with.'

Sophie grinned at him as she followed through

the gate. 'Of course. Claire and Briony have given me all the riding gear they no longer wear, and I've got those lovely R.M. Williams boots you and Ginny bought me.' She held out a foot. 'I reckon these old boots of Briony's will do for travelling. I plan on keeping the new ones for impressing my new employers.'

Kirk guffawed. 'I don't think new boots will impress them—but I'm sure you will.'

'Aww. You're really a softy, aren't you—under that beard.' Sophie reached up and gave his beard a light tug.

He wrapped an arm around her slight shoulders. 'We'll miss you, kiddo.'

'I'll miss you too.' She swallowed the lump that attempted to form in her throat as Ginny caught up to them.

'Come on, you two. Sam will be waiting—and so will everyone else. Briony said Eleanor's heading off this morning as well, so I expect there'll be quite a farewell committee.'

Ginny was right. As Kirk drew into the hotel car park, Frank, Lola, and Zoe were standing next to Eleanor's little grey car, sharing hugs. Zoe clasped a plastic container of lamingtons, seemingly patiently waiting for the chance to hand them over.

Sam slid the cover back on his ute, exposing a storage area already half-filled with his backpack, camping fridge, the new canvas swag everyone had chipped in to gift him, and an esky full of food.

Briony and Alex appeared, and everyone seemed to talk at once, rotating around the three departing friends as though they were heading to the moon.

Eventually, Sam and Sophie were seated in the ute, Eleanor was ensconced in her little car, and the cavalcade moved slowly out of the car park.

'See you at Christmas,' Ginny called.

'We love you both,' Claire added.

'Don't forget, this is your second home!' Briony waved frantically as she yelled the words, and Sophie bit back the tears that threatened to flow.

THE FOLLOWING DAY, the morning of Naomi's court hearing, a thin veil of fog shrouded the town of Emerald as Sam and Sophie continued their journey to Cranwell Station. Flatly refusing to allow Sophie to be collected by her new employers, Sam had insisted she obtain directions to the property and that he would deliver her in person.

'What if the place is nothing like what you're expecting and the people are horrible?' he said.

Sophie laughed but agreed, secretly delighted that Sam was so caring and protective.

They were less than ten kilometres out of Winton

when Sam's phone rang, it's tone loud and demanding as it vibrated through the ute speakers.

Sam flicked a thumb against the steering wheel button with the picture of a tiny telephone on it. 'Hello.'

'Gidday, guys. How's the trip going?' Rhys's friendly greeting put a smile on both their faces.

'Great,' Sam said. 'We're on our way to Cranwell Station now. Stopped and checked out the hotel I'll be working in first.'

The phone crackled as Rhys's voice broke up.

Sam pulled to the side of the road and switched off the ignition. 'Sorry, mate. Missed that. We've stopped now, so go ahead.'

'I thought you'd like to know how Naomi's court hearing went.'

Sam faced Sophie and grimaced. 'Yeah. How did she plead?'

'Guilty of all charges. The story's interesting though. She told the court she only took Ciara's passport because Ciara and her boyfriend were going to buy drugs from someone they all knew. It seems Ciara and Naomi had hooked up while travelling in Ireland as people thought they were twins. What began as a joke, became a concern for Naomi, who reckons she didn't realise Ciara was a hardened junkie—thought she just used recreational drugs like herself. Anyway, whoever this guy was that she met in

Ireland caught up with them again in Glasgow. Naomi swore in court that Ciara left with him to go to a party and didn't take any of her belongings. When she failed to return after two days, Naomi took her passport, phone, and bankcard, supposedly planning to keep them safe until she saw Ciara again. That didn't happen though, and Naomi's story was that she "thought if she didn't take Ciara's stuff, someone else would have".'

'Jeez. Taking someone else's passport and travelling halfway across the world with it is not exactly looking after it though, is it?' Sam's eyes widened in disbelief as he faced Sophie. 'So, what else happened?'

'The British police are presuming Ciara is dead, although no body has yet been found. Because of that, no charges can be made against Naomi as there's no proof that Ciara didn't give her permission to take care of her passport and phone. Naomi's charges include bringing stolen goods into the country and also fraudulently obtaining money by deception. She swore her drugs were for personal use only so hasn't been charged with dealing. The court has taken into consideration the month she's been in custody, so she'll have another two months inside before being released on a twelve-month good behaviour bond. Her passport has been confiscated so she can't leave the country and she'll be on weekly reporting conditions to a probation officer in Brisbane.'

'That's a relief. Now I can effectively cut her out of my life,' Sam said.

'Yep. I reckon it's time you make the most of your time in Australia—and we'll see you again soon I hope. I'd like to have the opportunity to flog you again at tennis.'

Sam exploded with laughter, and Sophie giggled.

'I'll let you guys get on the road again. Sam, make sure you look after Sophie or you'll have the whole of Featherwood Falls to answer to.'

'Huh.' Sophie snorted. 'You make me sound like a five-year-old.'

They laughed again and finished the call.

They had driven another few kilometres before Sam spoke. 'We know Rhys was joking ... but I want you to know I really enjoy your company. You're a beautiful person.'

Sophie glanced at him. 'Thank you. You're not too bad yourself,' she murmured. 'We both need a friend, and I admit I wouldn't mind ramping up our relationship. But it's been a turbulent few weeks and ... well, one step at a time?'

'Sounds good to me.'

His grin widened as they slowed beside a wide property entrance with a long, engraved sign propped metres above the road on steel posts. The name glistened in the late afternoon sun. "Cranwell Station."

Sam reached out a hand and clasped Sophie's. 'We're here.'

36

After throwing herself on the bed late that night, Briony propped herself on an elbow and stroked Alex's cheek with the back of her hand.

'Who would have thought this little hotel could have so much happen within its walls.'

He chuckled. 'You're right, lass. It's not quite the little café we thought we'd set up in, but it certainly has come with an interesting history—and I've no doubt it will continue to have an interesting future.'

'What did Sophie say when she rang?'

'Umm. Debbie and Mark are nice.' He reached out and turned off the light before pulling the doona up to his neck.

'And?' Briony blinked in the dark. 'What else?'

He sighed as though preparing for Briony's inquisition. 'The house is enormous—she reckons the verandas are four metres deep and wrap around every side. They're screened and have enough beds on them to sleep twelve people without having to use any of the five bedrooms inside.'

'She doesn't have to sleep on the veranda, does she?' Briony didn't even try to keep the horror from her tone.

'No. She's got her own little place outside—called it a "donga", whatever that is.'

'You've seen them—there's one in the corner of the schoolyard here in Featherwood Falls. Where Ashleigh lived before she and Damian built their house on the farm. They're what Australians call those portable cabins that are dotted all over the country—great for short-term or staff accommodation on properties and places where it's hard getting builders.'

'Yeah. Anyway, she's got one of those but will be having her meals with the family.'

'Okay. Is that it?'

'She'll ring us in a couple of days and tell us more.'

Briony released a long breath. Alex was tired. They were both tired. Accepting she would have to wait until morning to drag more information from her weary partner, she pressed her body against his, drawing his warmth into hers as the old hotel groaned under the rising wind outside, and they drifted into sleep.

~

As though in tune with Alex and Briony's moods, heavy grey clouds hung over Featherwood Falls the following morning as the wind howled, buffeting leaves along the roadside.

After the hectic weeks prior to the opening party and Eleanor's, Sam's, and Sophie's departure, Briony wandered aimlessly around the deathly quiet hotel.

By midday, with no guests or table bookings for the evening, Briony tentatively picked up the phone and punched in Ann's number.

'Hello.' Her voice chirped brightly, and Briony released a relieved breath.

'Hi, Ann. How was your weekend?'

'Great, thanks. Yours?'

They chatted for a few moments before Briony gathered the courage to divulge the real reason for her call to this no-nonsense woman. 'I know it's only Tuesday and not one of your usual days for working with us—but I wondered if you'd mind doing a few hours so Alex and I could have some time away from the hotel?'

'Pfft! Of course I wouldn't mind. Nothing to keep me here and it's about time you two gave yourselves a break. What time shall I pop down?'

'One o'clock? There are no bookings for dinner yet and we can deal with the lunchtime pop-ins. We'll be back in time to do dinner.'

'If there's no reservations for tonight, why don't you

forget about the pub for a few hours and make the most of your time off? I'll manage—have done it plenty of times before,' she finished with a brash snort.

Briony grinned. As a long-distance truck driver, Ann's husband was rarely home, and with her experience as a shearing gang cook and their grown family now scattered around the country, Briony suspected her hours at the hotel filled an empty spot in Ann's life.

'Thank you, Ann. I appreciate your help.'

'Goodo. See you then.'

The minute she ended the call, Briony rang her sister.

'Hey there.'

'Hi, Claire. Have you got any riding students today?'

Claire grunted. 'No. School holidays are over, remember? No kids except at the weekends now. Why?'

'Ann said she'd come and look after the pub for a few hours, and I thought it would be nice if Alex and I could go for a ride over the farm. We haven't had a chance to get away for ages—and even then it was only to buy essentials for the hotel.'

'Of course. I'd come with you except I have a design project to finish. Lola and Frank are coming for lunch, so why don't you join us then go for your ride?'

'Ann will be here at one so if Mum doesn't mind holding off until then, we'd appreciate it.'

'Done.'

'Thanks heaps. Alex will be chuffed. He's pressure-cleaning the beer garden.'

'Boring,' Claire drawled in a singsong voice.

'I know. Has to be done, but I reckon "blowing the cobwebs away" from the back of a horse will go down a treat.'

Laughing, the girls ended their call and Briony dashed outside to tell Alex.

THE RELAXED MEAL surrounded by family and special friends was everything Briony needed. Although she and Alex adored the hotel, the view from the homestead across the fields and valley was hard to beat and one Briony never tired of.

'Sophie rang Alex last night,' Briony announced.

'She phoned me too.' Ginny grinned at her daughter. 'And so did Sam.'

'Oh! I wonder why he didn't ring us?' Briony frowned, a little peeved that he would call her mother before Alex or her.

'He will. It was just a quick call as he was unpacking before he had to do a familiarisation of the place with one of the other guys.'

'Is everything alright?' Alex asked.

'Yes. He seemed happy. Said he liked Sophie's new

employers. Apparently, the property is like nothing he's seen before—huge, red dirt, and mostly flat, which he's not used to. He didn't say much about the hotel except it had a nice feel to it and is surprisingly busy. I think he was more concerned about Sophie.'

'He's a kind soul,' Lola said. 'One of those salt-of-the-earth blokes who lost his way for a little while, thanks to Ciara's manipulative ways.'

Ginny nodded. 'He is. Said he'll bring Sophie back here for Christmas, so of course I told him he was welcome too.'

Kirk chuckled. 'I reckon he'll be a completely different Sam by then—a much happier one.'

'Eleanor phoned too,' Lola said. 'She had a good trip back to Brisbane and is now waiting for word from the police about releasing her sister's remains. I guess that'll be the catalyst that will confirm whether or not she sells her Brisbane apartment and moves. It seems she's now giving thought to having a new house built here if she can't buy something.'

'Good grief. She's an energetic eighty-five-year-old to be taking on that challenge,' Kirk said.

'I reckon now she has so much to think about—and what with having Timothy as a friend—she's keen to delve into more genealogy and experience what it might have been like for her parents living out here. Of course, she's also met all of us and believes she was meant to return home to Featherwood Falls.'

Ginny pressed a hand against her chest. 'That's so beautiful. Imagine living eighty-five years in Brisbane and then choosing our little village to spend the rest of your life in.

'I can think of plenty of worse places,' Frank added drily.

'I agree.' Briony pushed her chair back and stood. 'Come on, Alex, let's get these horses saddled before our precious time off runs out.'

WITH ALEX MOUNTED on Splash and Briony riding Akela, they cantered across the wide ridge at the back of Featherwood Station before halting at the top-most peak where the pasture ended and the native bushland began.

'Oh, I've missed this.' Briony turned to face Alex, her cheeks flushed pink and her hair loose under the helmet. The gloomy air had cleared, leaving a vibrant blue sky filled with puffs of scudding white clouds.

Alex beamed, the lines around his eyes creased and the stubble on his chin shining gold in the afternoon sun. 'Now the hard work's behind us, I think we should get better organised so we can have a day off more often—every week if we can.'

'I agree.' Briony pointed to the boundary between Featherwood Station and Glenrowan. 'Let's head down the fence line. We can check the windmill and troughs before visiting the falls.'

Alex nodded, urging Splash into a brisk trot as they rode side by side.

When they reached the windmill, they dismounted and let the horses drink.

Briony sat on the edge of the concrete trough, dipping a hand in the water. 'This is one of the horrible things Nigel messed up to frighten Mum.'

Alex frowned. 'It was a tough time for her. Featherwood Falls has certainly had its share of rogues.'

'Yes. And pretty much every other type of crime over the years, just like most places if you delve deep enough. I guess discovering Ciara's offenses just added another couple.'

Alex rested an arm over her shoulders. 'Come on, love. Let's forget about the past and focus on the future. Race you back.'

Laughing, they both mounted hastily and galloped across the paddock before halting at the gate with heaving breaths.

HALF AN HOUR LATER, with the horses tethered to the red gum tree, they stood facing the waterfall as it gurgled and tumbled its way down the slope into the pool and spilled over the edge to continue down the valley.

'This is my favourite part of this whole farm.' Briony's dreamy gaze drifted from the top of the peaks above them to the village below where the water continued past the bottom of the hotel garden and under the bridge at the edge of the town.

'I agree. It's hard to beat.' Alex moved to Briony, and they held each other, her head resting on his shoulder. 'I love the hotel and Featherwood Falls is about as similar to living on Skye as we can get—only a whole lot warmer.'

Briony squeezed him tightly. 'So, you're not going to change your mind about us staying here?'

'No. This is where we'll marry—soon I hope. And I'm happy to live here for as long as we can. Agree?'

'Absolutely.' Briony tilted her head back as the sun kissed her face. 'Although I've loved travelling and especially living in Scotland, it's good to be back home.'

'Then so it will be—our home.'

EPILOGUE

*B*irdsong filled the air. With the bright sky above and the spring sun slanting through the trees, Briony scrabbled for her sunglasses and clasped Alex's hand as they joined the group encircling the tiny grave.

Eleanor and Timothy stood with Ned, flanked by Lola, Frank, Ryan, Emma, and Zoe, while both Ginny and Kirk chatted with the vicar. A few locals drifted in to join the group, but there was no sign of either Rhys or Claire, causing Briony a sliver of anxiety.

'They said they'd meet us here, didn't they?' she asked Alex.

'Don't worry. Rhys probably got a phone call as they were about to leave the station. They'll be here shortly.' He ran a finger inside the front of his collar, as though attempting to loosen the unfamiliar tie Briony had insisted he wear.

'We're the owners of the building where the poor little girl was born, died, and was buried,' she had said. 'Anyway, we don't know who else might be there—like a reporter or someone who might want to take a photo for the newspaper.'

Alex had nodded and done as she suggested. And now the time had come to put the child to rest for a second time.

On the dot of ten o'clock, the vicar welcomed everyone before proceeding with a brief introduction, a prayer, and opening a hand toward Eleanor. She adjusted her glasses and read from a sheaf of folded papers, beginning with a summary of her search for family connections and ending with the discovery of the baby and the link between the two of them.

'I would now like to honour my sister with the farewell she deserved over eighty-five years ago and lay her to rest in her rightful place here in Featherwood Falls. May the sun bless her with warmth and the angels look upon her. One day, we will be together again.'

Briony swallowed. The sadness in Eleanor's voice evoked memories of the loss of her own father, and reminded her of Ciara's parents in Ireland, waiting for news of their daughter.

Instinctively recognising Claire's presence a metre

away, she turned, raising her eyebrows at her solitude. 'Where's Rhys?' she mouthed.

Claire shook her head and lifted her gaze to the vicar.

'Thank you all for coming. Please join Eleanor and friends at the hotel for refreshments.'

Within minutes, he and Eleanor had shared quiet words, and he strode to the road, got into his vehicle, and drove away.

Briony and Alex stepped closer to the little mound of dirt in front of them highlighted with a small head-stone engraved with two doves and the name "Baby Johnson", 19 April 1939.

Ginny bent and placed a posy of flowers in front of the plaque, and they stood for quiet minutes before Lola touched Eleanor's elbow. Then they turned and led the party toward the hotel.

IN THE DINING ROOM, a spread of cold meats, salads, and savouries waited, and while Ann served drinks to the small crowd, Rhys rushed through the door, his hair like a porcupine's and his hat under one arm.

Briony raised her eyebrows. 'Emergency?'

He shook his head. 'Tell you after lunch.'

Intrigued, Briony bit back further questions and urged everyone to help themselves and have a seat.

The pub hummed with conversation until, with the meal over and those outside the immediate circle of family and friends drifting off, Rhys cleared his throat. 'I'm sorry to bring you bad news on what has already been an emotional day for some of you but thought you might like to know we've received advice from Interpol about Ciara.'

Everyone stilled as a frozen silence filled the room. They gathered closer.

'The authorities have confirmed the identity of one of two bodies found in a remote area of Yorkshire, England as Ciara King—the real Ciara, that is. The other was a male person, believed to be Ciara's boyfriend. Investigations are continuing around the cause of their deaths, but at this stage, the suggestion is a drug overdose.'

'Does Sam know?' Ginny asked.

'Yes. I've given him Ciara's parents' address and phone number as he wants to ring them and share his condolences.'

Briony's shoulders heaved. 'At least they now have answers, even if they're not what they wanted to hear.'

'Yes. I'm sure. And it's very thoughtful of Sam to want to phone them.' Ginny looked at Alex. 'Have you spoke to Sam or Sophie this week?'

Alex smiled gently. 'Not for a few days. It seems this is a busy time of year with new foals arriving and cows calving. Sophie is loving it—and says she's slowly adjusting to the heat. Sam gets a couple of days off per week and has been going out to the farm to help too.'

'So the romance is blooming?' A knowing smile spread across Lola's face. 'I thought it might.'

'Yes, and they'll both be home for Christmas ...' Briony took a deep breath, 'and our wedding.'

Lola clapped and rushed forward, grasping Briony in a hug. 'That's wonderful news. Would you like me to make your dress? Or the cake? Or both?'

Briony giggled and raised her eyes at Alex. 'I warned you—weddings in Featherwood Falls are a community affair.'

'This is our home now—so that suits me just fine.'

As though in agreement, a family of magpies on the fence outside stretched their necks and warbled, their melodic song bringing laughter to all.

Alex waved at them. 'Yep. Even the magpies agree.'

AFTERWORD

If you enjoyed this book, I would love you to leave a review on your preferred site. Reviews encourage authors to continue writing and also help other readers to find my books. Thank you for reading "Coming Home to Featherwood Falls".

ALSO BY HEATHER REYBURN

Tullagulla Series

The Cedar Tree

The English Oak

The Pepperina Grove

A Tullagulla Christmas

Fantail Ridge Series

Peninsula Promises

The Lupin Fields

The Scent of Promise

Featherwood Falls Series

A Stranger in Featherwood Falls

Secrets in Featherwood Falls

Sparks Fly in Featherwood Falls

Clouds over Featherwood Falls

ACKNOWLEDGMENTS

To my beloved husband and sisters, I value your encouragement, support and honest critique above all else and thank you from the bottom of my heart. Your suggestions, constructive comments and tolerance make the relatively lonely career of writing worthwhile.

To Anna and Lauren at CREATINGink, thank you both for editing my books. Your professional assistance and ongoing friendship is very much appreciated.

Patti Roberts at Paradox Book Cover Designs—thank you again for your gorgeous covers and so much more.

Readers, I hope you have enjoyed reuniting with the Featherwood Falls community in addition to getting to know Briony and the new faces in town.

Thank you for your ongoing support and encouragement - and for reading my books.

A STRANGER IN FEATHERWOOD FALLS

To lose a loved one is tragic, but to lose a lifetime of dreams? Unthinkable.

Alone on a two thousand hectare sheep and cattle property, Ginny Shepherd questions her husband's sudden death, convinced it was no accident. As a series of farm related incidents unravel, heightening her suspicions, her livelihood is put under threat. Featherwood Station is Ginny's lifeblood—her passion, her home, and her haven and she is determined it will stay that way. But it seems someone else wants the property as much as she does and will stop at nothing to get it.

When a stranger finds a forgotten token gifted to him as a child, distant memories set him on a path to pursue his grandfather's dream. But, greeted with more questions than answers, he finds life in the heart of

Queensland's Granite Belt more difficult than expected.

A smouldering attraction forms between he and Ginny, alarm bells sound and frightening events escalate. Ginny's life is in danger.

Is the stranger who he says he is? Or could it be that someone has a grudge to settle?

SECRETS IN FEATHERWOOD FALLS

A small country town. A conscientious cop. And a whole lot of secrets.

Constable Rhys Morton is new to Featherwood Falls and knows one thing for certain—he wants to remain in this village as much as he wants to remain a cop. But just as he uncovers troubling historical information, an accusation threatens his security and he must weigh up his options. Should he pursue the cold case and risk ruffling powerful feathers, or protect his future and a budding romance?

Claire Shepherd is still reeling from her father's death and when fresh heartbreak strikes, she seeks peace in the haven of Featherwood Station, her childhood home. Sparks fly between Claire and the new cop in town and she is torn between her dream of managing her father's legacy or falling for a man whose position is only temporary.

Alarm bells chime when new neighbours move in. Is this little town the sleepy hollow Rhys believed it to be? Desperate to uncover local secrets, he seeks Claire's help. After all, she knows the area and he has nothing to lose—except his heart.

Secrets is Rhys and Claire's story and the second in the Featherwood Falls series.

SPARKS FY IN FEATHERWOOD FALLS

Fed up with life under scrutiny, Ashleigh Paton considers her grandmother's favourite saying—*"Escape to the Country! A Change is as good as a holiday."*

The advice ignites a yearning in Ashleigh to leave city life and all it involves. A teaching position in Featherwood Falls could provide the answer, one she hopes will offer the new life she craves. After all—what could go wrong? It's better than being unemployed and the reward could be the peace she desires.

Damian Cartwright has a secret. Like his eccentric great-aunt, a reclusive life in the bush suits him. Except now his son, Charlie, is old enough to start school, and old enough to be subjected to ridicule. It's time for action, even if that involves calling a truce with Charlie's feisty new teacher.

When unexplained events occur in the area, young

Charlie forces Ashleigh into seeking answers. But uncovering the truth proves more shocking than imagined and sparks fly in more ways than one.

Can Ashleigh extinguish the inferno without destroying all she has gained? Or will her dreams be over before they begin?

Sparks Fly in Featherwood Falls is the third book in this series.

CLOUDS OVER FEATHERWOOD FALLS

In a town teaming with secrets, three women find themselves inexplicably entwined.

At the edge of her future, sixteen-year-old **Zoe** teeters, uncertain. The vibrant city with its dazzling lights, familiar sounds and scents, and close friends exudes adventure and a dream career. But when unexpected tragedy strikes, she is left to navigate the world on her own, gripped by loneliness and fear.

Lola is feeling the weight of her years. Despite a loving husband, a flourishing business and a circle of faithful friends, she's missing something. While she pours her soul into a menagerie of sick and abandoned animals, her heart aches for the return of her only child.

At forty-two and feeling lonely, **Emma** is free at last. Lost love and an unwavering commitment to her late mother have confined her to the quiet charm of Featherwood Falls. And while her role as teacher's aide at the local school fills her days, she longs for something to happen—something that will transform her existence and redefine her life.

Can Featherwood Falls offer the key to uniting these women? Or will a dangerous voice from the past destroy family bonds, challenging the discovery of love and hope.

ABOUT THE AUTHOR

Heather Reyburn enjoyed an idyllic childhood in beautiful New Zealand, before settling on the Darling Downs in Queensland. With a passion for nature, animals, reading and all things farm related, it wasn't long before her rural lifestyle inspired dreams of writing stories of her own. She loves happy endings, history, suspense, and characters who remain with the reader long after "The End". When not writing, Heather is often found in the garden or spending time with her husband and family.